RENOVATION OF LOVE

Love on Madison Island 1

MEKA JAMES

This story would not have been possible if not for Tasha L. Harrison and her wonderfully encouraging group The Wordmakers. Thank you all for not letting me give up on myself or this series no matter how much whining I did.

Thank you to the other members of my writing squad who've been with me from the start.

This story was also therapeutic because, seriously fuck cancer!

Cover design by Kylie Sek of Cover Culture
Illustration by Tamara Davies
Edited by: Tera Cuskaden

<u>Love On Madison Island</u>

Renovation of Love

Heat of Love

Mechanics of Love

Follow me on Bookbub for up-to date information about future releases

****CONTENT WARNING****

This story contains mentions of grief, cancer, sickness, and abortion. While none of it goes into great detail, it may still be upsetting to some readers.

CYNTHIA

T he crunch of gravel filled my ears as I eased my 4Runner onto the long drive, flanked on either side by the mossy oak trees that led toward Aunt Drea's house. The very house I'd inherited three years ago but hadn't been back to. It wouldn't be the same without my beloved aunt, and living over two thousand miles away made it easier to put it out of my mind.

Madison Island used to be home, and this place used to be my sanctuary. Funny how time changes things.

Memories of the summers spent here running around the five acres of land that backed up to the protected marshland flipped through my head. As I'd gotten older, I'd considered this home more than the actual house my parents had provided.

Because my career as a corporate marketing executive had been going well in Portland, I'd never imagined I'd return for more than a sporadic visit to see my aunt and friend. Even fewer after I'd moved Auntie Drea to Oregon with me. Unfortunately, a buyout and an "absorption of my position" abruptly sent me on this three-sixty life detour.

With a cloud of dust behind me and a hard screech of my tires, I came to stop in front of the large, three-story, weathered Victorian house, parking next to the sleek, dark blue Buick mini-

SUV. Regina—one of my best and longtime friends—smiled brightly in my direction.

She exited her vehicle as I did. "There's my girl," Regina squealed, doing a jog hop dance move around her car to embrace me.

"Hey, hey lady." I stepped back, holding my friend's hands at arm's length to look her over. I whistled through my teeth. "Whew, girl, you looking good. And pictures didn't do the color justice." I jutted my chin upward toward her hair.

The locs Regina had been growing for the last ten years were now colored a vibrant red, with her eyebrows matching. A bold look, but one she pulled off flawlessly.

"Thank ya, thank ya. Have I told you how happy I am you are finally bringing your ass home? Because I am. Yearly trips and video chats are not enough."

"Yes, I know. You've only mentioned it a couple million times at this point."

"Oh..." Regina ran back over to her car and returned with a lime-green box and travel coffee mug. She handed me the box. "For you."

A large grin spread across my face. "Are those what I think they are?"

I lifted the lid and inhaled the glorious scent. Apple fritters. I loved those damn things. Like, more than I probably should. Throughout all my years in Portland I'd never found any that were even as remotely as good as the ones from Regina's bakery. To be fair, there wasn't anything I didn't love from there, but the apple fritters were my absolute favorite.

"What better welcome home?"

"Gurl, I gained ten pounds just smelling them, but I'm going to enjoy the hell out of each one all the same."

I glanced back at the foreboding house. I couldn't believe I was here—and for good. After being downsized, I'd agonized over what was next for me. Initially, I was set on looking for a new position, but the low, burning anger at being let go after being loyal to my company for over fifteen years held me back. At forty-three, I'd been easily replaced by someone younger and with half my experience. And if that could have happened at a job I'd worked for years, the thought of putting in more of my time and energy at someplace new didn't sit right with my soul. Not to mention ageism being alive and well. I was closer to retirement than most companies would probably like, on paper at least. Another hurdle I wasn't sure I wanted to jump.

Regina squeezed my arm. "You okay?"

"Yeah...just, it's a lot. All of it. My job, this whole plan, and that." I pointed at the house. "It's not going to be the same."

"It'll be something new, something fresh. You're going to make her proud."

The absentminded habit I'd formed over the last three years played out. Without much thought, I reached up to close my fingers around the gold cross hanging from my neck. It was the only piece of jewelry I wore daily. Something of hers I could keep close and draw on for strength when I needed it.

Aunt Drea had been everything to me. The mother I should have had. Unlike my real one, who spent every waking hour reminding me how great her life would have been under different circumstances. My aunt had been my confidant. My friend. My biggest cheerleader. Convincing her to leave this place and move to Portland where she could get top notch medical treatment and I could look after her had taken some effort, but in the end she'd conceded. Plus, it was my turn to take care of her like she'd done for me over the years since my own parents couldn't be bothered. It'd been hard to watch her wither away as the cancer consumed her. She'd fought it to the end.

Being her only beneficiary brought up family drama like only deaths can, but in the end, my sorry-ass parents relented when they knew I wasn't selling, and I sure as hell wasn't letting them live here to ruin the place. Instead, I'd kept it empty for the last three years.

Regina had acted as caretaker. Her son had kept the grass cut before he'd moved, and she aired it out a few times a year. However, the neglect was starting to show. Some of the shutters were missing, the paint was peeling, and it looked like the birds had taken over the porch judging by the amount of deserted nests and poop. On top of the lawn being a bit overgrown.

I had my work cut out for me, but this place was going to be my new beginning. Something to call my own. And something I couldn't be downsized out of after fifteen years of fucking loyalty.

Fishing the keys out of my pocket, I linked my arm with my friend and headed toward my new, old home. "Hopefully the power is on. I called last week to have it connected. Same with the water and gas."

"I told you to stay with me anyway. Who the hell wants to live in a construction zone? You know I got the space, and since Darnell has moved out for college, the house is kinda empty. More so now that he plans to spend the summer with his girl-friend instead of coming home. Though I don't tell him that. He already be expecting me to drive my ass to Atlanta to feed him. Like the meal plan I pay for isn't enough."

I laughed listening to her fuss about her son. It was hard to believe that he was grown now. Really made me feel my age thinking she had a nineteen-year-old out of the house and living on his own at Morehouse.

"You're right, and I will be taking you up on it." Just the idea of living in a mess of dust and debris was enough to make my sinuses act up.

I unlocked the door, and it opened with a soft swoosh. Dry leaves swirled on the hardwoods in the foyer.

Home.

Being back in this place released all the memories I'd kept stored. The grand entrance where we'd taken our prom pictures. The beautiful mahogany stairs with the hand-carved banister. The dark wainscoting lining the walls. Such a difference from my nine-hundred-square-foot, two-bedroom, modern condo with views of the city. It had been small and efficient. And just what I'd needed.

This house was filled with character, and warmth, and coziness that had been absent from my life for so many years. My place in Portland had been the exact opposite of everything I'd grown up around. I'd wanted it that way. To be different. To be new. To be me—or who I thought I'd wanted to be. However, stepping over the threshold let me know I couldn't run from who I always knew myself to be.

Home.

But not. No calls from the kitchen asking if it was me or if I was hungry. No late nights watching TV eating stove top popcorn and drinking hot chocolate.

"Whew...it is a bit musty. Things have been busy at the bakery; I haven't had a chance to get over here." Regina headed off and started opening windows.

She went right toward the parlor; I went left toward the dining room. The furniture was covered with sheets. I hadn't the heart to sell any items, so everything was still here. Just as Aunt Drea had left it after we'd packed her belongings and closed up the house.

My heart squeezed. Eventually I'd get used to her being gone. Today was not that day.

In the kitchen, I opened the window over the sink. Already the house was feeling cooler thanks to the breeze from the marsh. Twisting the faucet, the pipes creaked and groaned before water came sputtering out.

"Ew, that don't look good," Regina said, peeking over my shoulder.

She was right, the brown, rust color that came pouring out was troubling. It could be due to how long the pipes had gone unused, or it could mean an issue with the plumbing. Something I'd have the contractor inspect whenever they got here.

"Yeah, I'll have it checked. What time is the first person due to arrive?"

Regina took a sip of her coffee and looked away. That was never a good sign and certainly meant she was hiding something. I'd leaned on her a lot during the move—having her research the zoning, getting the correct forms for applying for the business license—so I couldn't be too mad if she forgot or didn't have time to get the contractors set up. But my type A personality was a little pissed because I needed to get this started sooner rather than later. I knew this process could take months, if not longer, and I didn't want to overstay my welcome at her house while this place was under renovation.

"What did you do? Or not do?"

"Nothing. You always thinking I did something."

I arched a brow. Over thirty years of friendship meant I knew her all too well, even with thousands of miles between us.

"Because you always doing shit. Now, what's with that face?"

She set her cup down on the dust-covered butcher-block counter. "Look, so, there is only one crew in this town that I like to work with, so...I may or may not have only contacted them for the job. But listen...he's good. He's done work for me at the shop, and at my house. Not to mention him and his company did all the revitalization work on the boardwalk shops. I know you haven't been there in a while, but seriously our town is getting quite the facelift little by little. I wouldn't set you up with just anyone."

I crossed my arms and eyed her suspiciously. There was something to this, I knew it. "Okay, so how long you been sleeping with him?"

"What? Why...gurl, please. You wrong for that."

"Am I? The way you are setting me up here means it's something more than just a work thing. You are selling it too damn hard. So..."

She rolled her eyes. "I'm offended. I could just really like working with this man without knowing him in the biblical sense."

"You right. You could just like his work, but that wasn't a denial. That was more a maybe."

She put her hands on her hips and frowned. "I'm not even going to dignify your statement. Anyway, he'll be here in"—she checked her watch—"about right now. If nothing else, he's always punctual. And if you're nice, he might give you the friends and family discount."

"Uh-huh, and I'm supposed to think you aren't sleeping with him."

She swatted my arm. But again didn't deny it. I knew this woman, and there was a reason she wasn't saying who he was, or why she was so gung-ho to have me use him. I mean, her house and shop did look great with the updates she'd done. The bakery had been in her family since her great-grandmother, and she'd worked to modernize it but still keep the history of the space. I'd let her secret guy have his time to give me thoughts and tomorrow I'd research a few others.

Having options was the right thing to do. I didn't need just any old hack coming in, fucking up stuff, and then leaving the job undone. Or trying to price gouge me because materials might be harder to get because it's a small town or some other such nonsense.

The sound of a car door closing made us both look toward the front of the house.

"Told you, punctual." She picked up her cup and sashayed her ass out of the kitchen. She was out the door and I heard her greeting before I stepped over the threshold. "Hey, Marcel. How are you today?"

Who? Wait? This had to be a joke, right? But my eyes didn't lie.

Her silver mug gleamed in the sun from the hood of her car, but it didn't stun me as much as the action playing out. She wrapped her arms around his neck when he bent to give her a hug. This was her new guy? Her mystery man? I didn't understand the burning jealousy that shot through me at the idea of the two of them together. It'd been over twenty years. And I'd lost any claim to him when I'd left, but still...*my* Marcel?

All ability to process thought ceased in that moment. I ground my teeth together and concentrated on taking steady breaths. Regina was one of my closest friends, if they were dating, she would have told me. But still...Marcel. Whatever they said I couldn't hear over the ringing in my ears. I couldn't move past the spot I'd stopped. She spoke, he smiled then looked up at me, and my heart jumped into my throat.

If ever there was a man that was the embodiment of tall, dark, and handsome, Marcel Lewis was him. Even twenty-five years later, the sight of him made my stomach flutter. His dark-brown skin shone in the mid-morning light. Gone were the black waves he'd spent way too many hours brushing so they'd looked perfect, and instead his head was bald. But the beard? He'd had one of those from the minute the first whiskers sprouted. Thick, full, and sprinkled with gray. Fully grown-up Marcel was just as fine as the teenaged one I'd left behind.

"Hey, Cyn. Good to see you."

Fuck, even his voice. Deep, smooth, with a little gravelly undertone that always got thicker when he was being sexy. Or rather actually putting effort into coming off as sexy instead of his normal state of being.

I swallowed the dryness in my throat but couldn't make my feet move. I shot Regina an "I'm going to kill you" look and worked to gather my thoughts. How could she spring him on me with no warning? Some friend she was. Irene would never do such a thing.

"This is new. I don't remember you never having something to say." He smiled again, but this time it was the one that had sent horny teenage me into a tailspin. The crooked, lopsided grin that got him out of more trouble than should have been possible.

I pressed my lips together and pushed down those thoughts.

"Hey. I'm just...surprised to see you. Regina hadn't told me who her contractor extraordinaire was."

She again took a drink, glancing around and trying—but failing—to look innocent behind her mug, knowing she had done me wrong.

He looked down at her and chuckled. "Not much has changed with you two, I see."

"Nope, she's forever doing me dirty and claiming it's for my benefit."

"It is," she cried. "Marcel is the legit shit when it comes to construction. You'll be in great hands."

Yeah...I remembered how great his hands were.

"Thanks, Gina," he said and kissed her cheek.

That green streak roared to life again, and I stomped it down. My feet still refused to work, and I hoped my mouth wasn't open when he strolled toward me. The jeans he wore sat right at his hips, loose, but not baggy. I didn't understand why the slight rip at the pocket gave me a thrill, but seeing that white fabric peeking through had some ungodly feelings dancing a jig. A simple white tee was stretched across his chest and around his thick biceps.

Why did he still look so damn good?

I had to tilt my head up when he stood right in front of me. From a distance, I was already in awe. But up close? His rich chocolate eyes and full lips I remembered all too well were almost too much to process. Less than five minutes around him, and I was transported back to the past. Yeah, I was going to cuss Regina out after this. He opened his arms, and I shuffled forward for a warm but awkward hug.

"It's been a long time," he murmured.

Fuck, he even smelled good.

"Yeah, it has."

When he pulled away, I couldn't meet his eyes. We hadn't had a conversation since the night before I'd left. Even when I'd come back for short visits, we'd not ran into each other. It had nothing to do with me trying to keep the places I went limited to narrow my chances. Or, at least, that was the lie I'd told myself.

But there was no getting around it now, thanks to my traitorous so-called friend.

2

MARCEL

A month and a half. That's how long I'd had to get used to the idea of coming face-to-face with Cynthia again, yet seeing her still threw me off my axis. When Regina had called asking me about converting the place into a bed and breakfast, and zoning laws in regard to Ms. Drea's old house, I'd worried she was in charge of getting it sold.

I'd had mixed feelings when I'd learned Cynthia was coming back. It'd been something I'd hoped for one day so I could get some closure. Some real closure, not the fucking cowardly "Dear John" letter she'd sent me. Logically, it was something I should have been over years ago, but her abrupt departure from my life had remained a pebble in my shoe.

A lot of my wishful thinking had been wrapped up in the house. The fact that she had a connection here, something that could one day bring her back and I could get the answers I'd wanted for over two decades. It may not have been the most rational thing to hold on to, but some things couldn't be explained.

However, seeing her now, in the flesh, touching her for the first time since she'd ran off...so many thoughts whirled through my mind. And I was reminded of how much I'd missed her, more than I'd let myself admit in a long time. Two decades and a life-time lived, and I was still—at least partially—hung up on Cynthia Marshall.

"So," Regina said, coming to join us on the porch. "I'mma head out. Need to run some errands." She gave her friend a hug and a smile. "I'll see you at the house." She turned to me. "Talk to you later, Marcel."

And she was gone before either of us could say anything. We watched her drive off in a cloud of dust, and I was left alone with the woman who'd broken my heart. As much as I wanted answers—real answers—I was here to work, nothing else.

"Let me get my notebook and we can get started."

"Huh? Oh, yeah, right."

She stepped off the porch and followed me toward my truck. Leaning against the front, Cynthia folded her arms and stared up at the dilapidated Victorian. I remembered its former glory, and the restorer in me was eager to bring it back to its majestic state. I hoped her plan to turn it into a B&B wouldn't take away from the charm and historic features. None of the modernizing that stripped beautiful houses like these of all their craftsmanship in the name of new age living and open spaces.

I joined her, opened my notebook, and tried not to stare at her. She was older, but the same. Gone was the shoulder length hair she'd always had. Mostly at her mother's insistence. *A woman's hair was her crown.* The saying that Cynthia had mock-ingly repeated many times over played in my mind. Though, no matter how much she'd complained about the time and effort she had to spend on it, she'd kept it long to appease her mom.

The shorter style suited her well. A pixie cut—at least that's the term I'd heard Alicia call it when she'd talked about cutting her own hair—graced the gray strands Cynthia had started getting in high school. The soft silver color looked sexy on her, and she sported it with pride.

The faint laugh lines that surrounded her honey-brown eyes couldn't be missed. You'd think after twenty years and the way things were left, I wouldn't be as excited and entranced by her, yet, frustratingly enough, I was. But I wasn't here to think about how good she smelled, or how soft she'd felt in my arms.

"What are you thinking for the outside? Any changes?"

She was thoughtful for a moment as she appraised the place. "I think I'd like it back to what it was before. The same colors. Though the quick walk-through we just did showed that there will be some wood repair needed."

"I can handle that. Shall we go in?"

She nodded, and I extended my arm, indicating she should lead the way. It also gave me a chance to check out the view from the back. The cutoff jean shorts she wore did her all sorts of favors. Cynthia had always been shapely, and the years had been most kind to her. From the soft curve of her hips, to her round, high ass...not to mention her toned arms and full breasts accentuated under the fitted tank top. Yeah, most kind indeed.

I shook my head. Nope. If I kept looking and thinking things I shouldn't, this walk-through would get real uncomfortable real fast. Not what I needed to deal with at the moment.

"In here, not much to change. Again, cleaning up, replacing any wood that needs to be repaired," she said as we walked into the foyer.

Damn, this place brought back memories for me, so I could only imagine what being here without her aunt was doing to her. Ms. Drea was everyone's auntie. She'd loved having us teens around and gave us a place to hang out without being too parental. And some much needed privacy at times. It'd been nice, and I'd spent many hours out on that very porch, or in the kitchen. This place had been like a second home to all of us.

Home. Cynthia was home, and even though I'd had time to get used to the idea, I still hadn't allowed myself space to dissect what that meant to me. If it even should mean something. High school was nearly a lifetime ago. Two, in fact. I'd lived, loved, married, had kids. Did she have kids? Was there a mister that would arrive later? Regina hadn't given those details, but the thought of having to make decisions with some man who got to live the life I'd planned didn't sit well with me.

Again, I shook off those thoughts. Work. I was supposed to be working. Besides I'd gone on with my life and dreams; I couldn't begrudge her for doing the same. Or at least I shouldn't have.

Work.

"No painting the wood, right?" The hand-carved, deep-brown wood was beautiful even with years of neglect. I was sure there was termite damage, but I'd worry about that later.

"Hell no. Auntie would rise up from the grave and kick my ass if I even thought about covering all that up. I know light, bright, and airy is all the rage, but nope…" She ran her hand along the bannister, her eyes glazed over as if traveling back in time. "There's beauty in the original. In showing off what was handmade with love and countless man hours, no doubt. Screw light, bright, and airy. I want the charm."

A large smile spread across my face. A woman after my own heart. Too many times I'd talked with clients that were all too eager to "freshen up the place" by slapping white paint on everything. It nearly gutted me every time, but I stayed silent once I knew it was a lost cause and did the job I was paid to do.

"So, where do you see most of the work being needed? The major changes, since Gina said you're turning this into a bed and breakfast."

She nodded thoughtfully. "It was one of her dreams, you know. Auntie's. She'd said for years the house was too quiet when we all… Anyway, she never got around to it, but I will. For her. Plus, this is a new adventure in my life."

Left. When we all left was what I was sure she'd meant to say. I wanted to remind her *we* didn't leave, she did. Life wasn't the same. Being at this house wasn't the same. She'd set us adrift. Set me adrift. So much so, that I couldn't get away fast enough from the town I'd thought I'd never want to leave. But I pressed my lips together and kept those thoughts to myself.

"I'm sure she'd be proud of what you're wanting to do here."

Cynthia gave me a sad smile before turning and walking off toward the kitchen.

"This room will need some updates. It's small and I need it a little bigger. I don't want to take walls down, but at the same time it's the only way to get more space. I probably should have not scheduled this for the same day I got back. I haven't had a chance to walk through and get reacquainted." She squeezed her shoulders and huffed out a breath.

The natural instinct to pull her into my arms to comfort and calm her before the frustrations overtook was strong. It was no longer my place, and I needed to keep things professional. As much as I could anyway.

"It's okay. It's not like I don't know this place almost as well as you. We can work it out together." I bit my tongue to keep from saying the rest of my thoughts. Like, how we used to be a good team and could handle anything as long as we did it together. I'd thought for so long that was true, that we could take on the world. Until we couldn't.

"Right. Well, I think the biggest changes will be on the second and third floors. I want to make sure each bedroom has its own bathroom, which I know will take a lot of reconfiguring. And I want to make the third floor an owner's suite out of the attic. Like full-on apartment if that's possible."

I nodded and took notes, scribbling down ideas. Once we finished the walk-through, I took pictures.

"Okay, so I'll think over what we talked about. MJ will—"

"Who?" she asked, interrupting me.

Right. Considering she left and never looked back, I was sure she'd not been asking for updates on my life.

"My son, Marcel Jr. He works with me and does all these renderings on the computer, it's what he went to school for. He'll make up some 3D images of options on what the finished product could look like, and when we meet up again, you can look them over and decide."

An expression I couldn't place flashed across her face. Was it anger? Shock? Sadness?

"A son... I guess congrats would be too late in this instance, huh?"

"Just a bit considering he's twenty-two. I also have a daughter, Alicia. She's eighteen."

She nodded slowly. "Well, I look forward to meeting them both. And Mrs. Lewis," she added at the end, but in a way that sounded like a question. Was she fishing for information?

I smiled and shook my head. "Ex-Mrs. Lewis. But if we're on the subject of partners...do I need to wait until your other half shows up?"

We stepped onto the porch and she shoved her hands into her pockets. "You'd be waiting forever if that was the case. It's just me, myself, and I."

Her answer made me happier than it probably should have, but I did my damnedest to keep that reaction to myself.

"Okay, well, how about if I give you a call in a day or two?"

She crossed her arms and cocked out a hip. "Sounds like you're trying to get my number."

I folded my arms across my chest and widened my stance. "It's kind of hard to discuss details with a client without it."

She simply smiled and held out her hand. "How are your folks and the rest of the family?"

I placed my notebook and pen in her grasp. "They're doing well. Mom and Dad moved out to San Diego a few years back. Mom wanted to go back to a place with year-round great weather, and Dad figured she'd moved around plenty for them during his time in the military, he could do the same for her." The pang of guilt about how I wasn't as accommodating with my ex zinged out of nowhere.

She nodded and scribbled down her information before handing it back to me. "What about your sister and brother?"

I closed the book and tucked it under my arm. "Well,

Jennifer still lives here. She's married to Eddie and they have three kids."

Her eyes went wide. "Wait. Eddie as in Eddie King football star? Your best friend Eddie? How did that happen?"

I chuckled and rubbed the back of my neck. The fact that my buddy married my older sister was still a weird concept at times, even if they'd been together for more than fifteen years.

"Well, high school football star, maybe a little in college, but you know he got injured in a game?"

She sucked in a sharp breath. The surprised look on her face softened to concern. "Oh, no."

"Yeah, for a while he didn't think he'd walk again. Managed to do that and finished his degree. Now he's the district superintendent and she's charge nurse over at County."

Cynthia leaned against the doorframe; her interest in the family that at one time doubled as hers was completely genuine. We stood on her porch catching up like this was any regular day of the week.

"And Keith? What sort of trouble is he up to these days?"

"None. I wasn't the only one to follow in Dad's footsteps and go Army. Only he's made a career out of it. Currently stationed in Seoul. Married and has one son."

"Keith...wow. Never saw that coming. Um...with you, either. Military life wasn't for you. Or at least that's what I remember."

I pulled the handkerchief from my back pocket and wiped the sweat from my brow. "Yeah, well, this place wasn't the same after...Joining up seemed like a good way to get out."

Cynthia diverted her gaze and shifted her weight. One sentence and the reality of the current situation was slingshot back to the forefront.

"So, what about you?"

She frowned. "What about me?"

"What's been keeping you busy over the years?"

She stood straight and shoved her hands in her back pockets

while shrugging. "Not much. Work mostly. Loved my job in marketing." She took a long breath and her shoulders slumped for just a moment before she continued. Had she not left voluntarily? "And I spent time traveling. Went to so many amazing cities and countries. There is a lot of world to see. Once the business is up and running, I want to continue. There are places I haven't checked off yet."

Long before she'd disappeared like a thief in the night, Cynthia had always had dreams of seeing what else was out there. Stars in her eyes for wanting to experience different cultures, ways of life, wanting more than what our small town had to offer. What *I* had to offer.

I swallowed down the painful truth. "I guess the pressure's on to get this project finished for you so you can get back to being the great explorer." I meant the last part as a joke, but with the way her face scrunched I didn't think it landed right. "Alright then, I'll be going." I jogged down the three steps and strolled over to my truck. "It's good seeing you again, Cynthia."

"You too, Cel."

The use of my old nickname crossing her lips brought a grin to mine as I climbed into my truck and drove off.

 3

CYNTHIA

"Irene, tell her she was wrong for what she did," I said over the speaker of my phone.

Regina walked around her island to where I sat and refilled my wineglass. Her smug grin and haughty attitude made me want to throw something at her.

"That was pretty low, Gina. You could have given her a heads-up."

Irene, our other friend, raised her own glass over the video chat, the attitude coming through the screen in waves. She had a knack for it.

"You know if I had, she would have given a million and one excuses not to see that man despite him being damn good at his job. Or worse, she would have kept her ass in Portland and scrapped the whole idea." Regina gave me a pointed look, calling me out as only a friend who was more like a sister could.

"She's right, now that I think about it," Irene chimed in.

"Seriously, both of you are supposed to be on my side."

Not that there were sides to take. Marcel and I were ancient history. An ex-wife and two kids type of history. Yet, seeing him today—just like being at the house—had turned back the hands of time. His comment about joining the Army rattled around like a marble. He'd left and from what he'd implied, it was because of me.

Regina took a sip of her Chardonnay. "We are. You know he's the town's most eligible bachelor, right?"

I shook my head. "Irene, get your friend. I'm here for y'all and the house. I ain't got time for no man. Especially not that man." And especially not if it meant drudging up the past.

"I don't know why not. Have some fun. You know it's like riding a bike, only with better thrills."

Irene screamed a laugh through the phone at Regina's lewd statement. She moved just out of reach when I went to swat her arm.

"I can't with you. With either of you. Wrong. Just plain wrong."

Irene leaned forward and the screen showed the call was paused. A few seconds later, her mood had changed.

"I gotta go, girls. Derrick just got home."

We barely got to say bye before she disconnected.

"There is something going on there," I said, draining the last of my wine before reaching for the bottle.

The attitude change in our friend had been a slow progression for the last few months. Abruptly getting off calls. Mood shifts when we'd ask how things were going with her and her husband, or really even asking about him. They were a rock-solid couple. The "Joneses" as it were. Something was up.

"I agree, but she'll say when she's ready." Regina got up to retrieve another bottle. "So, are you really pissed at me about not telling you?"

"Yes! How could you set me up like that?"

"Because if I didn't you wouldn't have met with him. Catching you off guard was the best way."

I knew she was right, but I still didn't like it. During the months leading up to my final decision to move back, the biggest hang up I had was living in town with my parents again. Being across the country made it much easier to avoid them and the stresses they brought to my life. But in the back of my mind there was also the possibility of facing Marcel. He'd been an off-limits topic for so long. I hadn't wanted updates; I couldn't handle them, and my friends had respected that choice.

But it also meant I'd been too stubborn to bring him up to Regina during my decision-making process. There had been a slim chance he'd have moved away—which he apparently had—but knowing how much he'd loved our hometown, I had more of a feeling he'd still be around, and I was right.

"Besides, what happened, happened and I doubt he's been holding a grudge for twenty-plus years. It's not like he's been sitting around pining away for you or some shit."

I slapped the granite countertop. "Yes. About that. Two kids and an ex-wife."

"Whew, chile. The lord might strike me down because MJ... Sweet Jesus, that boy. Not gonna lie, I have to remind myself that Darnell is not much younger than him."

I stared at my friend and pulled the bottle closer to me. "Okay, no more wine for you."

"I'm just saying. Marcel's genes are strong, but mixed with Porsha's, that boy is too pretty for words. His daughter is a knock-out, too."

Porsha. I kept the snide remark about being named after a car to myself. I didn't even know the woman, but it sounded like my friend did. Pumping her for information would be wrong, but at the same time, I wanted to know what kind of person Marcel had walked down the aisle with. Not that it was really any of my concern. She'd given him what I wouldn't. And regardless of what Regina believed, I'd gotten the distinct impression Marcel had in fact held onto a grudge or something for the last twenty years despite being married.

"But I only look, don't touch. Besides, I ain't got no time to be teaching some youngin' how to sex me." She ran her hands down the sides of her curvaceous body and did a little sway. "This fine-tuned machine needs experience."

My eyes went wide for a split second before I burst out laughing. "You are a mess. A whole, hot fucking mess and I love it."

"Love you too, girl. I'm so glad you're back." She wrapped her arms around my shoulders and squeezed.

This was what I needed. To be here with my friend and begin a new adventure. I'd enjoyed my time in Portland and had built a nice life there, and a mixed network of friends, but it was not on the level of what I shared with Regina and Irene. Sonya, who'd lived in the unit across the hall from me came the closest. We'd do dinner and shows together. Complain about work, and generally had fun when we'd hang out. I'd miss her the most.

Other than her, my friends there were separate groups. I'd had the work friends and my hiking friends, and they didn't overlap. Each group provided a benefit, but I was a different version of myself with each of them. None of them got the full picture of me like my homegirls did. It's not to say I didn't enjoy time spent with my friends there. I did, but it was never quite the same.

In Portland I'd stayed more reserved, but being back, surrounded by those who knew me best, I could simply be, and I'd missed that. For better or worse, Madison Island was my home, and at the end of the day coming back made sense. But being home meant dealing with Marcel in a much closer way than I'd expected. Nor was I prepared for the onslaught of old emotions returning at the sight of him.

❧

THE SMELL of freshly brewed coffee pulled me from my slumber. I groaned and rolled over to grab my phone. Seven a.m. But if Regina was just now making coffee that meant she was getting a late start at the bakery. Something that was unusual for her as she needed to oversee everything.

I tossed the covers back and gave my body a good stretch

before standing, wincing at the pops and creaks of my old bones. After a quick trip to the bathroom to take care of business and brush my teeth, I padded down the hall. I could have almost been one of those cartoon characters floating in the air following a scent as my nose led the way. Cinnamon rolls had joined the glorious coffee aroma.

"Hey, hey."

"Shhh…not so loud," Regina groaned before taking a sip from a black mug. "Why you let me drink so much?"

I walked over and filled the matching cup beside the coffee maker. "Don't blame me if you still can't hold your liquor."

"You're just a terrible influence."

I blew her an air kiss.

"Anyways, pull the rolls out in five. I need to jump in the shower and hope the marching band leaves my head so I can get to work. Lord knows, Trent may burn down the place if I don't get there soon."

I laughed at her dramatic statement. If there was anyone she trusted with her bakery, it was Trent. He'd been her second in command for at least the last seven years, but Just A Bit of Sugar was the one area Regina was majorly serious about. She liked to joke around and have fun, but when it came to the family business it was all work, no play. Four generations strong and a town staple.

I made my way over to the oven and opened it enough to check the cinnamon rolls. They smelled divine. In a marbled wooden bowl on the counter was her homemade icing. Man, how I'd missed this. There were plenty of food places in Portland, but nothing that compared to the creations Regina and her family produced.

Glancing around, I located the oven mitts. If I let these burn, she'd never let me hear the end of it. I'd just finished icing them when she walked in dressed in bubblegum pink scrubs with cookies, cakes, and other treats all over them. The store name and logo were emblazoned on the right upper side. Her locs were in a partial up-do with some in a bun on top and the rest hanging free with a matching scarf tied around her head. She completed her look with bright fuchsia lips and a sparkling light pink eye shadow.

"Do you make the staff all wear those?"

She looked down at herself. "Yes. They like them. In fact, we held a contest, and everybody voted. We have three different sets, but everyone likes working in the scrubs. They're comfy, have pockets, and not restrictive. Anyway, I gotta run. Lock up when you leave and then stop by the bakery. Momma has been blowing up my phone asking when she's gonna see you even though you just got here yesterday. That woman..."

She gave me a quick hug and was out the door. I plated one of the rolls and took it and my coffee over to the island. As I ate, I looked around and really took in the place. I'd been here plenty of times but never paid close attention. Knowing Marcel had done the work made me take notice.

My gaze was drawn to the hood range first. It was a honey oak wood with panels running down the front in a craftsman style to match the cabinets. Along the lip were stunning carved flowers with intricate vine work that ran down the curved arms, making it look more like a piece of furniture rather than what it was. Had Marcel done that, or did she buy it? I made a mental note to ask.

He'd been intense when he talked about the woodwork and the little details. I hadn't remembered him being into carpentry before, but time had passed. He was into different things now, which shouldn't have come as a surprise. Being in Portland had turned me into a semi-outdoor enthusiast and an amateur photographer—two things I never imagined I'd be into. But moving across the country alone was the perfect opportunity to try new adventures. And that was what I'd wanted. Adventure, excitement, new experiences. All the things I knew I wouldn't have if I'd stayed in Madison. *If I'd stayed with Marcel.* My breath momentarily caught in my throat.

The Marcel I remembered had wanted to be a teacher, possibly coaching the high school baseball team. He hadn't had dreams of grandeur like me, saying mine were big enough for both of us. But he'd had wants and desires which I'd known I couldn't fulfill. Some had changed. Owning his own construction company, being so into restoration...it made me wonder what else might be different about the boy I'd left behind. Like joining the Army as a way to...I shook off the thought before it could fully form, and carried my dishes over to the sink, rinsed them, then loaded them into the dishwasher.

Eyes on the prize, and head in the game. Marcel and I were past, and while he may be helping me with my present, that didn't mean a reconnection of what we'd had.

After showering and getting dressed, I knew I needed to head back to the house and get reacquainted with it. But first, the bakery. Driving the streets of Madison was like being in a time capsule. Sure, some new businesses had popped up, but for the most part it remained the same. Storied homes led to the downtown square where most of the action happened.

I couldn't stop myself from wondering if Marcel had done any of the work on some of the ones which gleamed like new. How much of the town had he put his stamp on? I tightened my hands on the steering wheel, twenty-four hours back and already Marcel Lewis was weaving his way into my every thought.

Instead of heading to Regina, I found myself taking a turn away from the city center and heading to the boardwalk. I may have lived on an island, but I'd never been a fan of the beach, however I had an unexplained need to see more of what he may have done.

A few of the simpler cottages closer to Madison Beach now sported second floors allowing the occupants better access to the views. The shops along the main throughfare were all coordinated in various shades of blues, greens, and yellows. I had to admit the updates gave the area an upscale feel while simultaneously maintaining the cozy nature you'd expect in a sleepy coastal town. The updates would work in my favor where my business was concerned.

And Marcel was responsible.

Continuing back to my original destination, I headed to the bakery. Just A Bit of Sugar had the prime location. A corner storefront on Main and Oak. Rumor had it that the lead city council member at the time was sweet on Regina's great-grandmother and she won the bid for this location even though it wasn't the highest. Knowing the women in her family, I could almost believe the tale to be true.

As I parked, a figure none other than my mother, Mary Marshall came strolling out of the bakery. I found myself slouching in my seat, hoping she wouldn't glance in my direction. Her dark hair was styled to perfection, and as usual, she was dressed as if she were going out on the town rather than to work for eight plus hours at the salon: in her slingback heels, fitted capri jeans, and a sparkling silver shirt that gleamed in the sunlight.

I continued to watch as she smiled and waved to people as she walked toward the beauty parlor, switching her hips and drawing all the attention she could. I stayed in my car until she was out of sight. Once it was clear, I let out a breath and rolled my neck before getting out and walking to the bakery. I knew I couldn't avoid her forever, but I wasn't ready to deal with the force that was my mother just yet.

The little bell above the door dinged when I entered. A giant chalkboard decorated with colorful font listed out the cakes, cookies, and other items available for the day. The large glass display cases were filled, and the sweet scents alone made my mouth water.

Behind the register stood Mama Charles, whose weathered smile grew wide when she spotted me. "Is that my little Cyn-Cyn?"

I simply shook my head, and the grin tugging at my lips couldn't be stopped. Small-town life. It didn't matter I was forty-three and fully grown, nicknames stuck even if they no longer applied. She came from behind the counter, and I welcomed her warm embrace.

"The one and only, Mama Charles. And why are you here working? I thought you retired."

She pulled back but held onto my hands. "You know that friend of yours can't do nothing without me. Besides? What you expect me to do, sit around and knit like some old lady? I'm too young and sexy for that." She winked with that last statement, and I could only laugh.

Her daughter was just like her. That apple didn't fall too far from the tree. She motioned to the young woman who had taken her place behind the register and then led me over to one of the metal bistro tables near the window.

"Is that... Tricia?"

Mama Charles turned around and nodded, a wistful smile on her face. "Yup. Going to that fancy culinary school in Savannah but working here to learn the ropes. She's next in line."

The pride in her granddaughter rang clear and true. It'd been some years since I'd seen Regina's niece, especially since Regina's sister had moved off the island after she'd gotten married. Knowing that generation five was coming up strong had to make them all happy.

"So, back for good I hear?" Mama Charles asked, getting readjusted on the metal chair.

"Yes, ma'am. Going to turn my aunt's place into a B&B. Gina has offered to come on board to provide breakfast treats, so we need to work that out."

She was thoughtful for a moment. "Ah, yes. I do remember her saying something about that. It's good. Most people stay over in Savannah when they come down this way, so getting some tourist business will be a boost."

Yes. I've done the research. Even stayed at a few different B&Bs to get a feel of how they're ran and made a plan. It'll be rocky because new territory, but I'm ready to give it my all."

Tricia brought over two lattes. "Here you go."

"Tricia, you remember your auntie's friend Cynthia, right?"

She drew her brows together and shook her head.

"Child, this is who Regina was talking about, the B&B."

Her eyes widened. "Oh. Right. Sorry."

"It's all good. I've been gone for a while. But I hear you're next in line to take the helm."

Tricia nodded. "Hope I keep it going strong like those before me."

Mama Charles squeezed her arm. "You're gonna do fine, baby."

Another customer came in and Tricia excused herself. For a Saturday, I expected it to be busier, but it was mid-morning and folks around here got much earlier starts.

Mama Charles took a sip, then straightened up when she looked at me. "Your momma was just here."

I took a drink of my own to buy some time before nodding. "I know. I saw her leaving as I parked. Stayed in my car." I glanced up with a rueful smile. On the rare occasions I would visit my parents it was because Aunt Drea would guilt me into it.

Mama Charles sucked on her teeth while straightening a little in her chair.

"Is she still always wanting a discount while barely being cordial when asking for it?"

Mama Charles rolled her eyes and pursed her lips. "I don't want to speak bad about your kin."

"It's alright. It's nothing I don't already know."

Before she could say anything, Regina emerged from the back with a white apron covering her uniform. She wore a frown, and the moment her mom saw it, she stood. Regina waved in my direction before signaling for Mama Charles to join her. Something was going on, and it didn't seem good. I said quick good-byes and promised to stop over for dinner.

The comment about my parents brought up the memories from the last time we'd spoken face-to-face. My mother had been pissed at the reading of the will, and surprisingly, so had my father. Everyone had thought they were getting a piece of the small pie Auntie Drea left behind, but other than a few knick-knacks and furniture items that had been heirlooms, everything had been given to me.

Because for all the talk she'd done about family, she'd known the one we were born into were pains in the asses on a good day. Even Pop-pop, a "man of god" had acted up. Going on and on about it being un-Christian like to not give to the church. That some tithes should have been left.

All of them had been pressuring me to give them something. My parents had treated me like my existence was a burden for most of my life, but I'd suddenly had value to them. My mother's comment especially on how I needed to show gratitude and give back after everything they'd done for me. As if I'd owed her... them for giving me life no matter how oppressive that life had been.

I hadn't even had the strength or desire to argue with them. Instead, I'd gathered my purse and the envelope that had contained the keys to the house, Aunt Drea's safety deposit box, and all her financial documents, then left. I didn't look back and damn near had been ready to block all their numbers when the calls kept coming weeks later.

Seeing my family was low on my priority list. I was juggling enough stress with getting the business off the ground, and the man in charge of helping me make that a reality.

❀ 4 ❀

MARCEL

Two knocks followed by the door opening signaled my son's arrival. MJ strolled into the kitchen with a travel coffee cup in one hand and his laptop in the other.

"Good morning, old man."

"Old. Please. You and I both know I can still take you if needs be."

"Yeah, yeah, so you say."

The relationship with my oldest had always been relaxed. We toed the line of being more like friends, but with respect in place. He was a good kid and working together had brought us closer. When I'd gotten out of the military, returning to Madison and making a life here had been high on my priority list. It was also the beginning of the end of my marriage.

MJ appreciated my hometown, my sweet baby girl not so much. She was more like her mother in that regard, so I'd done plenty of traveling back and forth to accommodate. I'd never wanted either of them to feel like I was no longer part of their lives. I'd always wanted them to know they were my priority no matter where I lived. Their mother and I had been divorced for longer than we were married, but I'd still had a strange moment of guilt assigning him work for my ex-girlfriend.

I'd spent all night thinking about Cynthia and the fact we were going to be living in the same town again. *Maybe.* She was starting a new business, but that didn't necessarily mean she'd be running it herself. Though I couldn't imagine her leaving anyone else in charge of her aunt's house. But if you'd asked me twenty-five years ago if I thought things would have ended like they did I would have said no, so it was clear I didn't know her as well as I'd believed.

Crazy how the years had gone by but somehow it still managed to feel like only yesterday since she'd walked out on me.

MJ put his stuff on the table and tilted his head. "What's that look?"

"What look?"

"Um, that almost dreamy look you have right now?" He walked over to where I stood leaning against the counter. "What's in that cup?" He raised my hand and took a sniff. I would have snatched it back if I wasn't worried about burning myself with the hot liquid.

"Boy, you know better. And there isn't a dreamy look on my face. I'm just thinking about the new project. The old Victorian we're not only restoring, but also renovating into a B&B."

He pulled out a chair, and I winced as he dragged it across my hardwoods instead of picking it up. He would be buffing out any scratch marks left behind.

"Ah, yeah, the place that's been vacant out on Henderson for years. How much work will it need? And can we take it on right now?"

I rubbed my hand over my head as I joined him at the table. When he'd expressed interest in being part of the business, I was proud. I had always hoped he would, but at the same time I wanted him to find his own path in the same way my father had encouraged me to find mine. MJ didn't love the down and dirty aspect of construction and preservation like I did, but still he had a knack for it. However, he excelled on the planning side. The rendering and imagining how the space would be after the work was completed. Luckily, we had a good crew and were like family.

"Well, we'll have to figure out how to make the time for it. The Bates' project is our only big job right now, and we have only maybe another three weeks. The Carter project is minor, and we won't need the full crew there. Besides, the owner is a friend so..." I took a sip of my coffee and left the order hanging in the air.

He nodded and pulled his laptop closer. "Well, I did a few renderings from the pictures you sent, but not sure if it's exactly what they're looking for."

A few keystrokes then he turned it to face me. He swiped through the options, giving the details of what was happening with each one. Some required opening more walls and completely changing the floorplans in a way that would strip the home too much. I ruled those out, knowing that Cynthia would agree with me. Or at least I suspected she might agree. He'd made six different models, and I narrowed it down to three.

"Shouldn't we ask the client? You're vetoing stuff like it's for you."

"We could, but I know this woman, Junior. She'd agree with me."

He rolled his eyes. "You always think people will agree with you."

"Because I know what I'm talking about."

He made a noncommittal noise and closed the lid. I knew he wanted to spread his wings and take on a bigger role, but he also didn't have the same appreciation for the older places. He usually got to run lead with those clients that wanted to take the old homes and make them look like sterile hospitals on the inside. It made no sense to me, but I didn't have to live there.

"When will we meet up with this woman you know all so well?" He rested his arms on the cherry wood table I'd made in my shop and gave me that look. The one that told me he again got our roles reversed and he felt it was his duty and right to pry into my personal life.

"How long you here for?"

He hit the screen on his phone to bring it to life. "I told Jerry I'd meet him at eleven. The Bates' is taking longer since they don't want us starting too early or working too late." The annoyance in his voice was easily detectable.

I understood it as their schedule requests were slowing things down, but they were okay paying a premium by taking up more time than necessary.

"Okay, let me call her to see if she can stop by since it's only nine thirty. You can show her and then leave if she's not made a decision."

"Or you could be wanting to kick me out so you can give this client *personal* attention."

I gave him a hard stare that only made him laugh instead of being the warning it was supposed to be. Both him and Alicia had amped up their mission to marry off dear old Dad. Or at the very least get me dating. They were under the impression that I needed more companionship in my life outside of wood and Clyde the betta fish.

I got up to retrieve my phone from my bedroom and dialed Cynthia's number. As I punched in the Portland area code I wondered if she'd change it to a local one, or would she keep it, like one foot remained out the door for another quick exit. She answered on the third ring, stopping the wayward train of thought from going off track.

"Cynthia Marshall."

"Marcel Lewis," I replied, matching her strange hello.

She was silent for a beat. "Oh, hey."

"Hey. You always answer your phone that way?"

"What way?"

"So professional?"

"Um, I guess old habits die hard. I used this phone for work and would get calls…anyway sorry about that. Good morning, Marcel, it's a pleasure to hear from you. Is that better?"

I smiled at the hint of amusement in her voice. "Yes. You been away too long, forgot how us small town folks do things." I wanted to take the words back soon as they were out, but there was no recall.

"Did you call to simply discuss my phone etiquette?"

"No. If you have time, maybe you can stop by to see the renderings MJ has for you. If you're wanting to move forward that is."

"Stop by where?"

"My place."

"First you conned me into giving you my number, and now you're luring me to your house."

I laughed softly. "Why are you working so hard to make this out to be something unsavory?"

"Eh, if the shoe fits. I know you, remember?"

"You *knew* me," I corrected. "Anyway, can you take down the address?" I added quickly before either of us could make anything out of my statement.

When I re-entered the kitchen, MJ was scrolling through his phone. "She'll be over in a bit."

I picked up my mug and dumped the remaining contents, washed it, and put it in the dish rack. I scanned the surroundings, making sure everything was in place. I didn't know why it mattered, but presenting a clean area was important.

MJ leaned closer to me and sniffed.

"What in the hell are you doing?"

"I don't know, old man, you were back there for a while. Thought maybe you were putting on cologne and making yourself all pretty," he joked.

I scrubbed my hands down my face, smoothing my beard as I went. "She's a client, nothing more."

He leaned back in his chair and crossed his arms with a

smart-ass smirk on his face. "I know you like these old places, but I don't know, Dad, you seem to be extra excited."

I chose to ignore his assumption, but I practically jumped out of my skin when my doorbell rang ten minutes later. MJ's laugh echoed behind me as I headed toward the door. There she stood in a light pink T-shirt with a V just deep enough for a tease of her cleavage but nothing more. The khaki shorts hugged the curves of her hips, and my fingers itched to pull her closer. Her silver hair was brushed flat, minus the deliberate swoop of spikes on top. And a hint of mauve tinted her full lips. Memories of the nights spent making out and kissing them threatened to make me act.

I mentally chastised myself. That kind of thinking didn't do me any good. "I see you found the place okay." I stepped to the side and let her in.

A soft floral scent trailed behind her. It was a mix of cocoa butter and roses. And it was amazing, like eating cookies in a field of flowers. I had to stop myself from audibly inhaling.

"Yeah, it's amazing how easily I'm recalling streets. I guess there really isn't any place like home. No matter how long you've been away."

"Possibly. Returning had been easy for me as well. Almost as if I'd never left."

She glanced up at me almost as if she wanted to reply, but instead smiled while keeping whatever thoughts to herself.

Focusing on her mouth brought back my desire to kiss her. I cleared my throat and took a step back. "This way."

Work. She was a client. No matter what the increase of my heart rate said, nor the uncomfortable tightening of my pants.

CYNTHIA

I TRAILED BEHIND MARCEL, AND I COULDN'T HELP BUT NOTICE how good his ass looked in the jeans. They weren't the ripped and rugged ones like yesterday. Instead, the dark wash with faded coloring on the thighs matched the light blue T-shirt he wore. It hugged his torso like the white one, and I was jealous of the fabric getting to be that close to him. I'd be lying if I said I wasn't a little disappointed about not getting a hug as a greeting.

When we entered the kitchen, a young man with Marcel's same dark complexion but lighter brown eyes and amazing cheekbones stood from the bar height table. I could see what Regina's drunken inappropriate comments last night were about. He rounded the piece of furniture with a smile all too familiar and his hand outstretched.

"Cynthia this is my son MJ, MJ meet my old...friend and our new client."

Both MJ and I glanced at Marcel as he stumbled over the "friend" part of the introduction.

"Nice to meet you, MJ."

"Likewise." And being every much as a gentleman as his father, he pulled out a chair for me to sit.

He grabbed the silver computer and sat next to me; Marcel

pulled a seat around and sat on the other side. I was flanked by the two Lewis men and utterly distracted by the older one. The younger Lewis launched into a spiel about the designs and laying the groundwork explanations about the images he pulled up.

"I made six, but Dad assured me you'd only be interested in these three."

I turned to look at Marcel and raised my brows. "Oh, he did, did he?"

Marcel stretched his arm along the top of my chair and leaned back in his. "Well, yeah. After talking yesterday, I think I have a pretty good idea of what you want. But...I've been wrong before."

I wasn't sure if that was a general statement, or a dig at me and how things were left, but I chose not to engage. Especially not in front of his son.

"Let me see all of them, but don't tell me which are your father's picks."

MJ did as I asked. The first three made too many drastic changes and I'd lose some of the woodwork in favor of making the downstairs more open concept. The remaining three kept more of the integrity of the house with minor differences in the floor plans based on how I wanted to change the kitchen and dining room areas.

It was easy to guess which were Marcel's top choices. I had to admit, the ones he was so certain I'd like did fit my idea better. I didn't know whether to be annoyed or in awe over the fact he actually did know what I liked after all this time. At least when it came to the house. My concentration was on the fritz being so close to him as we all huddled around the laptop. The brush of his arms, the heat of his leg pressed against mine, and the subtle clean scent wafting from him all messed with my head.

I was here to get this new business venture off the ground and start anew. None of my plans entailed rekindling a long-dead romance with the first and, if I were being honest with myself, only real love of my life.

Sure, I'd dated a handful of guys in college and an assortment of them during my time out west, but there had always been something that didn't quite click. My drive to do well in my career often became a sticking point. Even with my ex-fiancé—who had been just as career driven as I was—it suddenly became an issue when he put that ring on my finger. He'd been sorely mistaken when he'd thought three carats would turn me into Suzy Homemaker, but my refusal to cut back and think about being a housewife put an end to things two months before the wedding.

I pushed the thoughts back into the box of things not to be mentioned and forced myself to listen to what MJ said about the pros and cons of the options presented.

"So, what do you think, Ms. Cynthia?"

Oh, those Southern manners. I expected nothing less from Marcel's child. And it was another one of those minor details reminding me I was home.

"Hard to say. I think option two might work, but I need to spend some more time at the house. Can you email them to me?"

MJ rubbed the back of his neck. "Well, we typically don't..."

"It won't be an issue," Marcel spoke, interrupting his son. "I'll make sure he sends them." He stopped and smiled. "But I'll need your email address, of course."

MJ was already packing up his computer, muttering to himself.

"You keep finding ways to get my information."

"The more I have, the better it is for our working relationship." He stressed working, but the statement made his son look over at him, then to me, then back to Marcel.

"I have to get going," MJ said. "I'll get those plans to you as soon as I can." He gave his dad a hug, waved goodbye, and was gone.

I grabbed my purse from the back of the chair. "I should probably head out, too."

I was still rattled from being alone with Marcel yesterday.

And the closeness from the meeting was doing a number on my nerves, so I needed to get out before I said—or worse—did something I knew damn well better than to do.

He crossed his arms in front of his wide chest. "In a rush to leave?"

I slung my purse onto my shoulder and planted my hands on my hips. "Are you going to keep making snide comments? If so, maybe I should get other bids if this is going to be a problem."

It probably would have been easier to find a property in Oregon or surrounding areas to do this since Portland was too expensive. Though the market there was slightly more saturated regardless, making it harder to get a foothold. No. Coming back was my best option to make this work, but dealing with Marcel and his apparent unresolved issues wasn't something I had accounted for and wasn't sure I could handle.

"It's not a snide comment. It was a question. If you see it as more, then that's on you."

I pinched the bridge of my nose. He was right. This time. But the other little things. Though I could have been blowing those out of proportion as well. It was just a lot in a short amount of time, and my patience was nil.

"Look, Marcel. We have stuff between us. I get that. But it was a long time ago. We can get through however long this will take, and then we can go back to how it was before."

It was a bullshit statement. Being around him for a day proved why I worked so hard to avoid him in the past. The man before me was special. The connection and safety I had with him had never been replicated with any of my other relationships. And I knew part of that was on me. I'd never fully committed in the same way. Maybe it was fear of karma and having someone walk out on me like I'd done to him. Or maybe it had been my way of atoning.

He stepped closer crowding my space. I didn't want to look up at him, but I also wasn't doing myself any favors staring at his chest and imagining the muscles beneath the fabric.

"Which before would that be, Cyn? The before when we were a thing? Or the before when you ran off and became damn near a ghost for two fucking decades?"

I pressed my lips together and lifted my gaze to meet his. Dark eyes with a stormy expression knocked the wind out of me. And left all words locked in my throat. He lifted his hand but balled it into a fist before shoving both into his pockets.

He took a step back. "Text me your email and I'll have MJ send the renderings to you."

I simply nodded and followed him to the front door. He held it open and I started to speak but didn't really know what to say other than a generic, "See you later." He'd been so hurt by my departure he left the town he'd loved. I couldn't ignore that truth now that I knew. For so many years I'd told myself he'd be better off without me. That's how I'd gotten through the worst of it. I'd been steadfast in that belief, but one day back and he had me questioning it.

6

MARCEL

THE MOMENT I STEPPED INTO JUST A BIT OF SUGAR, MAMA Charles smiled and waved as she rounded the counter. I bent to give her the hug I knew she'd want.

"Marcel Lewis, coming to finally propose to me?"

I laughed. Even at sixty-eight, Mama Charles was the biggest flirt. Kept her young, she said.

"You'd only tell me no. Why would I set myself up for heartache like that?" I winked.

"Mm-hm. You never know. Today might have been your lucky day."

"Maybe, but I also know how many shotguns Mr. Charles keeps. I like all my limbs, thank you."

She laughed and swatted my arm. "What'll it be?"

I wasn't really in need of any pastries, though taking some to the worksite would give the crew a boost. I'd hoped to maybe find Cynthia here since, other than a text, we'd not talked for the last two days.

"Just give me two dozen mixed of your doughnuts, please. The crew could use the sugar rush."

"You probably could use a little sugar yourself. You seen

Cynthia?" She looked at me over her glasses when she asked the question.

One she probably already knew the answer to. Small town life. Everybody knew your business. Always poking around in things that really weren't of their concern. Though I supposed I should be thankful that there seemed to be one secret that hadn't found its way to the rumor mill.

"Yes, ma'am, I have. I'm going to be working on her place."

A playful smile tugged at her lips and she again peered over her glasses at me. "That all you working on?"

"Momma!" Regina came bursting through the double swinging doors. "I'm gon' have to fire you if you keep being the town gossip."

Mrs. Charles waved off her daughter and continued filling the green box with my requests. "You can't fire somebody that ain't getting paid."

Sometimes those two acted more like sisters rather than mother and daughter.

"You want a coffee as well, Marcel?" Regina asked.

"Nah, I'm good."

She came from behind the counter and pulled me over to the corner, away from her mother's prying ears.

"What'd you say to my friend?"

"Nothing. You brought me in, remember? I simply have a job to do."

She pouted and folded her arms across her breasts. At five-two, she was a lot of woman in a short package. And her bark could be nearly as bad as her bite if she was pissed. Even standing nearly a foot taller than her didn't deter her from trying to boss me around when she felt like it. Most of the time it was good natured and all in fun.

"Don't give me that look," I defended. "I'm here because of you."

"Right, because I'm trying to help you out, but you want to go and be difficult."

I suppressed a groan and tried to tamper down the quickly rising annoyance. The situation I faced wasn't all that unique. The friends were close, so them knowing the ins and outs of most things was expected. A lesser intrusion than general small-town life. Though I had to give it to Regina, of the two women closest to Cyn, Gina had been the one who'd worked hardest to soften the blow after Cynthia had bailed. Irene cared, but not in the same way. Not that either of them were responsible for trying to make the shitty situation better. They'd maintained their friend code, sticking up for Cynthia's choice, but at the same time trying to make me understand it wasn't personal.

Though it was hard for me not to take it personal when she'd left the way she had.

"I'm not being nothing. Just trying to get the job done. If I'm hired for it. No telling with your friend, haven't talked to her in two days."

She linked her arm in mine and led us back toward the pastry counter. "Oh, you're hired alright. I'm not letting her choose anyone else. And you better give her a good deal." She tugged on my arm, forcing me to bend so she could kiss my cheek.

"I'm charging her double," I said, handing a twenty to Mama Charles.

⚜

WHEN I ARRIVED AT THE BATES' site, I handed the box of doughnuts off to Mike. He was a young kid and the son of Jerry, one of my long-time employees. After Mike dropped out of college, his dad said he needed to find something constructive to do with his life and asked me to bring him on as a trial.

Helping out the youth was a passion of mine. Teaching shop and other carpentry classes at the local community center gave me fulfillment. College wasn't for everyone, and some who wanted to go couldn't due to circumstances. I was a firm believer that having a skill was useful. And put food on the table. Mike had caught on quick and was showing major pride in his work, much to his father's amazement.

Inside, I found my son talking things over with the tiler. Seeing Juan was always a sign we were close to the end. Just as I headed over them, my phone rang. Before I looked at the screen, I had a moment of hope it was Cynthia finally breaking her silent treatment, but it was Alicia's name instead.

MJ looked up and I held up a finger before sliding the green phone over to answer.

"What's up, Sweetpea?"

"Daddy, I'm eighteen. When will you stop calling me that?"

"Maybe when you're sixty."

I didn't need to see her to know she was rolling her eyes. "Anyway, can I come see you this weekend?"

That was never a good sign. It wasn't that I didn't love seeing my little girl. I did so as often as I could between work and her busy social calendar. But her calling and asking to come out of the blue meant she more than likely had another fight with her mother. Those two were too much alike for their own good. One minute they were as thick as thieves, the next it was damn near an outright brawl.

"What are you in trouble for this time?"

"Daddy." The whine in her voice mixed with the way she stretched out my name told me I was right.

"Don't 'daddy' me. Last time you pulled this, your mother had grounded you and you got me caught up in the middle."

"I'm an adult now, she can't ground me."

"Uh-huh, and did you risk your life by telling her those same words?"

"Maybe." Again she stretched out the words.

I chuckled softly. "Look, baby girl. You know you're always welcome. No question. But it'd be nice if you made these last-minute visits when you weren't having World War III with your mother."

"Thanks, Daddy. Love you."

I barely got to say love you too before she disconnected the call. I knew it'd only be a matter of time before Porsha called me.

"Was that Alicia?" MJ asked after I joined him.

"Yeah, how'd you know?"

"She's been blowing up my phone. Saying I left her to deal with Mom and I needed to call. The usual when she wants something and has been told no."

I ran my hands over my head and then down my face. There would be no relaxing in my workshop this weekend. Instead, it now would be filled with my daughter pleading her case for whatever it was she wanted in hopes I'd talk to her mom so she could get her way. Though, the distraction might be a welcomed one considering it would be better than replaying history.

"Speaking of calls, Ms. Cynthia emailed me back. She would like to see us whenever we're available. And by we, I mean you, because I don't want to be in the middle of anymore weird 'friendly' conversations."

So that's how she wanted to do this. "What do you mean weird? It was a conversation. That's all."

"Uh-huh. Right. Anyway, I told her *you'd* get back to her."

"With great power, comes great responsibility my son. You want to get more involved; client interaction is a must."

He laughed and started to walk away. "Whatever, I'm not trying to play chaperone with you two."

I stared at my son's retreating back. No idea what vibe he'd gotten from the short session with Cynthia, but I'd have to work harder at putting my issues aside when working.

❄ 7 ❄

CYNTHIA

I SAT ON THE BACK PORCH STEPS SIPPING MY COFFEE AND enjoying the peace of the property. It was nice to just have these moments of quiet, staring off at the marsh. The only noise coming from the squawking of the birds and croaks of the frogs. I made a mental note to ask Marcel about putting some sort of dock near the water's edge. It would be a nice place for people to sit and enjoy at the end of the day, or really at any time they wanted.

I set my cup down, leaned back on my hands, closed my eyes, and inhaled deep. The dewy early March air filled my lungs, grounding me. I loved the unique combination. A mix of freshly turned earth, with a mingle of saltiness. Being here made me slow down and just let myself be. It'd been non-stop planning, thinking, worrying. I *needed* to just be. As I took slow, controlled breaths my mind wandered back to the time spent on this very porch gazing out at the marsh under the moonlight. Stars twinkling overhead and Marcel...our first kiss as awkward and unsure as it was, had happened at this very spot.

The crunch of tires on the gravel drive followed by a slamming car door pulled me from my unexpected trip down memory lane. I took another deep breath and locked away the errant remnants of a life past before hoisting myself up, grabbing my cup, and strolling around the porch to go meet my contractor.

Marcel...I'd been avoiding him, again, but I needed time. Just a little bit to better steel myself and prepare to be around him. And to whip my wayward feelings under control. No matter how futile the attempt. How was it possible to be so drawn to a man after so much time apart? Two days wasn't enough, but I couldn't keep playing dodge Marcel. Not ever again with me replanting my roots in Madison. And especially not with him being instrumental in getting the renovations done.

There he stood in the bright Georgia sun at the back of his truck, buckling a tool belt around his waist. How in the hell did a man that worked around dust and dirt keep such a stockpile of bleach-bright white shirts?

"Good morning, Mr. Lewis."

He turned and smiled. "We're being extra formal now?"

I shrugged. "Where's MJ?"

"We need a chaperone?" The glint in his eyes coupled with the uptick of the corner of his mouth was a dangerous combination.

Yes. We probably did need one for a whole host of reasons. I took a swig of my coffee to steady myself before I said something I shouldn't and shook my head. "Just thought since it was his plans and all he'd be here."

He leaned into the open driver's side window and pulled out a black laptop. "I might not be as techy as the boy, but I can hold my own."

The slow, loose-limb gait of his was creating thoughts that had no place showing up. I spun on my heel and walked into the house to keep from staring. The words he'd spoken to me at his house had weighed on me. After this was done, which "before" did I think we could go back to? *Friends?* At the very least we should be able to call ourselves friends. That was how he'd introduced me to his son. And that's how our relationship had begun.

Classmates, friends, to so much more. The intensity and depth of feelings I'd had for Marcel had scared me as much as they'd comforted me.

"You told MJ you had some tweaks you wanted?" His voice boomed behind me and sent shivers down my spine.

I nodded, attempting to recenter myself. Sheets still covered the furniture in the front rooms. Ghosts of a past life. I knew I needed to make a decision: keep the stuff or sell it. But just like Auntie's bedroom, I couldn't bring myself to clean it out. I started to sit at the head of the large farmhouse table where many important conversations had taken place. The most important one over bowls of ice cream with scoops of support and love that only she could give me. But that was her seat, so I sat to the left of that chair with Marcel planting himself next to me. Too close once again.

"What changes?" he asked as he opened the lid to the computer.

I cleared my throat and tried to keep on track. "I think I need a business center. Nothing big, but people need to have a place to work."

"Doesn't that defeat the purpose?"

"The purpose of what?"

"Of what you want from this place. Getting the big city folk down to our little town so they can slow down." Deep lines marred his forehead.

"Yes, but even on vacation people still need to stay connected. And I should offer that barest amenity."

"It's not a vacation if you're working. Sure, give them Wi-Fi if needed, but a whole business center? They can stay at a chain motel for that. You've been gone too long, and it shows. You've forgotten everything and every—" He stopped and quickly rubbed his hands over his smooth head. "All I'm saying is Madison, your land, is special and has a lot to offer. More than you give it credit."

My chair made a loud scrape as I pushed back from the table.

There was more to that statement; I was sure of it. The unspoken underlying message was above and beyond our disagreement over a business center.

Marcel stood as well, his six-one frame seemingly sucking up all the space around me. He wrapped his calloused fingers around my wrist and pulled me toward the back door. The screen slammed shut behind us, bouncing a second time before settling. With his hands on my shoulders, he stood behind me, facing the very same view I'd been admiring when he arrived. Heat radiated off his body and I had to stop myself from leaning back against him. He squeezed and relaxed his grip in a gentle massage that I wasn't sure he was aware he was doing.

"Slowing down and enjoying the small things in life is what you should be focusing on. Small-town life isn't a prison. It's not something to escape for what might be bigger and better. There is happiness to be had here. You just have to want it." The tenor of his voice was low with a hint of melancholy. Again, the message was there as the word I'd used in my goodbye letter to him was repeated. Prison.

I'd needed to leave. To get out and away from this place. From him and those terrifyingly intense emotions I'd had for him and our relationship. To change things so history didn't repeat itself. Becoming my mother had always been my worst fear, and leaving kept that from happening to me. To us. I'd loved Marcel, and he sure as hell had loved me. But from the moment the test had turned positive all I'd thought was we would be like my parents. Teenagers that got caught up and were forced to deal with the consequences. And hating each other for it.

It would have been a lie to say I hadn't thought about Marcel over the years. I had. It was hard not to. Especially near the end when Auntie was urging me not to end up like her—alone. She'd never been the same after her divorce, and facing her mortality had allowed her to open up about it. Her fear of rejection, of being seen as having "no use" because she couldn't have children had kept her from being willing to fall in love again. She'd closed herself off and surrounded herself with us teens to act as surrogates to fill that void.

But playing the what-if game did me no good. I couldn't change the past, and being hung up on it served no purpose. So, I'd worked, and that had fulfilled me. However, facing that what-if in his chocolate-brown eyes was a game changer. And one I wasn't sure how to handle. What I did know, running wasn't an option this time.

He had a point. When I'd done my recon missions to other B&Bs I couldn't recall seeing a dedicated work area at any of them. They focused on recreation and highlighting the relaxed nature. A more intimate location as it were, different from the chain hotels. Madison was a beautiful place. I couldn't deny that. And I needed something to set me apart, my aunt's property was it. I should celebrate that and the town.

I stepped away and turned to face him. "So, no business center. Do you think you can build some sort of platform close to the marsh? I thought it might be a nice area where guests could sit and take in the beauty. And, as you said, enjoy all we have to offer."

He shoved his hands into his pockets and the bobble of his Adam's apple was visible before he nodded. "Yeah, with some lounge chairs. It'll be a good spot."

I pressed my lips together and turned back to face the water. It would be good. I could do this. I would succeed. And in an odd twist of fate, I'd have Marcel by my side as I made it happen.

MARCEL

I TRIED TO IGNORE CYNTHIA STANDING ON THE PORCH IN A dark green tank top and a pair of body-hugging capri yoga pants. It was too damn early in the morning for her glorious form to be sending my mind on a one-way trip to Gutterville. Curvaceous hips and shapely legs. Topped off with a smile that had no business making me warm like a ray of sunshine. It always had. Her smile had been the first thing I'd noticed about her when we were younger. Bright and genuine, it'd pulled me in.

First day of work on her project, and while I expected her to pop in to check on things, I didn't think she'd be here from the start. Nor did I expect her to want to help. Though not sure why. Cynthia had always gone out of her way to be helpful, to show she was useful, to prove she had a purpose for simply being. As a teen, she'd spearheaded the town's Meals on Wheels program. Organizing the haphazard practice of taking food to the people on the sick and shut-in list. All to get approval she'd never admit to wanting. The familiar anger over how her parents were flared up quickly, but I stomped it down. It wasn't the time or the place to rehash her dysfunctional home life.

After giving instructions to the crew, I sighed then grabbed an extra crowbar and sledgehammer from the back of my truck. "You know this is going to be nothing like you see on TV, right?"

She simply smiled then moved the mask dangling around her neck over her nose and mouth. Hitting things would certainly be an outlet for the slew of frustrations I was handling of late.

The symphony of banging, shouting, and cussing was already underway when we entered the house. MJ was heading up the work on the second floor, opening the walls and checking the electrical and plumbing before we could make a final determination on what the old house could handle as far as turning the third-floor attic space into her owner's suite.

That left us to tackle the beginning work in the kitchen.

"Okay, molding off first." I handed her the crowbar and the hammer from my tool belt.

She looked at the two pieces in her hands then back up at me. With her eyes alone, I knew she was probably cussing me out in her head while waiting on further instructions. After sliding my own gloves on—more to protect myself from the electric feeling of touching her skin—I placed my hand on her shoulders and turned her toward the doorframe.

"Like this." I stepped closer, wrapping my arms around her so I could control her movements.

Sure, I could have simply shown her by doing it first, but my brain ignored that logic and opted for putting me more in harm's way, so to speak, by being close to her. Playing puppet master, I placed the crowbar hand by the wide frame and then made her other lightly tap it just enough to pull it free from the wall.

"You have to go slow and steady," I said, leaning close to her ear. Her shea butter scent filled my nostrils, and it took an amazing amount of self-control to not kiss the small space of flesh. "Too rough, and you'll crack it. Take your time, be gentle and..." Three more taps and the piece pulled free.

Keeping control, I moved her arms lower, the change of position forcing her to bend. As a result, the ass I'd been taking every opportunity to stare at pushed into me. I nearly groaned from the contact.

"Be good to the wood, and it'll be good to you."

She looked back over her shoulder, her eyes glimmering with amusement. It could have been an accident, but she wiggled her fine ass against me with the next taps to break loose another section.

"Like that?"

She won that game of chicken as I took a step back before she knew exactly how good she'd been. Yeah, I needed to punch holes in something to keep my hands busy.

"One down, two more to go. Although I'll get the top piece. I don't want you trying that while on a ladder."

"Always trying to look out for me."

"I guess old habits die hard." She diverted her gaze and just that quickly the energy changed. "You finish that, I'm going to start on the appliance removal."

By lunch break, the crew had completely demolished the entire second floor minus one room. Cynthia hadn't wanted anyone taking apart her aunt's space. When I went to find her, that's where she was, leaning against the doorframe, looking almost too afraid to go in.

"You okay?"

She nodded without looking at me. "The last time I was in this room was when I packed up some of her stuff for the move to Portland."

Unlike the furniture that had been covered downstairs, a thick coating of dust sat atop every surface. I suspected that the door had been closed and it'd almost become a time capsule.

Ms. Drea had been a lot of things to all of us, but for Cyn, she was the mom she'd wished she'd had. It was no secret that Cynthia's parents had gotten married because Ms. Mary had ended up pregnant, even if such things weren't spoken out loud. And Cynthia unfairly carried the burden of that circumstance. Ernest Marshall stayed gone more than he was home, and Mary

Marshall had an amazing way of cutting Cynthia down while simultaneously playing the victim.

Her aunt had been a refuge. Her home a place where Cynthia's existence wasn't the root of all that was wrong in her parents' lives.

"Have you decided what you want to do in here?" I put my arm around her shoulder and she surprisingly didn't repel from my sweatiness, but instead leaned into me.

"I mean, it makes sense to let this be a room. The only bathroom on this floor is right next door, so logically... I just feel weird about people staying in this space. The whole house was hers, but to me, this was hers-hers. Ya know?"

In what used to be an all too natural move, Cyn slid her arm around my waist. When she glanced up at me, her golden-brown eyes shimmered with unshed tears. I wanted to cup her face and kiss her pain away. The sound of someone clearing their throat got our attention. MJ stood at the other end of the hall with a goofy smirk on his face. No doubt I'd have to hear more crap from him. He'd even gotten his sister in on the harassment when she'd visited over the weekend.

Cynthia and I broke apart when she reached to close the door to the room.

"Whatcha need, son?"

"Upstairs, have some things to point out."

Cynthia seemed to pay better attention as MJ laid out the pros and cons of creating what she wanted in the attic space. I couldn't get the memory of how she felt in my arms out of my head long enough to follow a complete sentence.

"What do you think?"

Both she and MJ were staring at me waiting on an answer to her question. Too bad I had no fucking clue what that was.

"Let me think on it and I'll get back to you tomorrow." I prayed it wasn't something simple I was putting off, but with them both nodding in agreement I seemed to be safe.

Sooner than I wanted, the workday wrapped up. Most of my

crew had already left, and there were only so many bullshit little things I could check on so that I'd be the last one there.

"I feel like I should buy you dinner after such a long day." Her voice sounded behind me as I took measurements for things that didn't really need them.

"Are you asking me out?" I teased.

"What? No... I mean it's late, I need to eat. You need to eat. No reason it can't be done together."

I put my tape measure back in the front pocket of my tool belt. "You do realize that unlike in the past, it's going to take more than pizza and a pretty smile to pay for my labor."

"So, beer?"

I barked out a laugh. "That's a start. I can meet you at Gina's. Or...you can come to my place. Your choice."

She sank her teeth into her bottom lip as she weighed her options. "I need to shower, but your place. Meet you there in like an hour?"

I did a mental fist bump. Not that I didn't enjoy hanging out with Regina, but having more alone time with Cyn would always beat that.

"Sounds good." And I was glad that came out sounding way cooler than I felt.

As I followed her out and waited for her to lock up, I was amazed at how much she'd turned my world on its axis again. It was almost as if that off-kilter feeling I'd had was righting itself.

9

CYNTHIA

"Where you going?" Regina asked as I held up a third shirt before tossing it onto the growing pile on the bed.

"Nowhere special."

She poked at the clothes scattered about before pushing the pile to the side and took a seat. "You can't be this damn indecisive about what to wear for nowhere special."

Our gazes met in the mirror and she wore a full on "don't bullshit me" expression with the pursed lips and narrowed eyes.

"Just having a celebratory-ish dinner with Cel for finishing a great first day of construction."

Her eyes went wide right before she scrambled off the bed and over to the closet.

"Stop right now. I know that look."

She waved me off. "Take off those jeans; this is a no pants night. You need a skirt. A short one. And the good underwear. Ohhh, and I need to call Irene. Our girl is getting back up on that stallion."

"First, it's dinner. Pizza. I don't need a skirt or the 'good underwear' cuz he won't be seeing it. Secondly, I'm not getting up on nothing, you nut. So, no calling Irene and dragging her into your foolishness."

She ignored me as she kept pushing my clothes along the wooden rod, looking for something she deemed worthy.

"This." She turned, holding my black wrap dress. "A little bit sexy, but not too revealing. Just a tease. Plus, it's easy to take off. It's perfect."

"No, ma'am," I replied, shoving my arms through the sleeves of the simple purple button-down. "I'm not entertaining you."

"Fine. Maybe playing hard to get will work." She spun me around to face her and quickly undid a button. "But not too hard."

I didn't even bother fighting with her.

"Oh, one more thing." She ran from the room, and I rehung the discarded shirts. "Here." She shoved a row of shiny foil packets at me. "He might have his own, but you should always go packing just in case."

I looked at the row of condoms. A row. Not one—the whole row of four. What the hell did she think I'd be doing to need that many? Or any?

I pushed her hand away. "Woman, please. I am having pizza without a side of Marcel."

"Please, you know damn well that man is a whole meal, with seconds and dessert. I remember how you talked." She tilted her head, arched a brow, and twisted her lips to the side. Then she walked over to the nightstand where my purse was and dropped them in.

Regina's overly enthusiastic and way off base impression of the night still managed to fill my stomach with jitters. Sure, we'd joked around some, and I didn't know how I even concentrated on removing the frame when he'd showed me how. His hands-on instruction approach was a distraction at best, a direct bolt of lightning to my long-neglected libido at worst. Much more of it, and I would have been begging him to toss me up on the counter and make me remember old times. Would he be expecting what she'd implied? I pushed the idea away as I pulled into his driveway.

This was a simple meal shared between friends. Nothing more. However, something stopped me when I started to close up the button Regina had undone. Okay, so maybe I wouldn't be too mad about something more possibly happening.

The door swung open no sooner than I'd rang the bell. "I thought you'd stood me up."

Not a hint of humor showed on his face. The gruff, flat statement told me my tardiness had hit a nerve. The same nerve that had brought out other hints of hostility. The niggling bit of guilt pricked in the back of my head.

"No, sorry. Got caught up talking with Regina."

I stepped in and was hit with the fresh, clean scent coming off him. Soft and subtle like a hot summer day after a rain shower. He was dressed for complete comfort in another one of those impossibly white T-shirts and shorts. Cotton shorts that— Nope. Eyes up. Because if I wasn't mistaken, there was a distinct imprint.

"She can be a talker. Pizza is already here." He extended his arm toward the kitchen.

On the way, I noticed a fish tank I'd somehow missed on my last visit.

"That's Clyde. The kids gave him to me a year ago, maybe two. A prank Father's Day gift. They have jokes about my bachelor lifestyle. So, they got something to keep dear old Dad company."

A curiosity that served no purpose returned. Who was the ex-Mrs. Lewis, and why were they no longer together? Was it something he did? Or her? The questions swirled, and I couldn't stop them from tumbling out of my mouth.

"How long were you married?"

He rolled his tongue along his bottom lip. "Eleven years. We got married not long after I finished bootcamp and divorced shortly after I got out of the Army. I seem to have a knack for picking women that don't like small-town life."

I pressed my lips together and released a slow sigh as the implication hung between us.

"And you? I know you said there isn't a current one, but is there an ex-husband you left behind?"

Another little dig. I swallowed down the instant retort and shook my head. "Just an ex-fiancé. I seem to have a knack for picking men that think I should pop out babies and be a homemaker."

His nostrils flared before he closed his eyes briefly and a fleeting, sad grin spread across his lips. "Actually, you don't."

Three simple words spoken so matter-of-factly because he was right. We both knew he was right. To a degree. But the degree to which he was wrong was one too big for us to overcome. I tried to ignore the skip in my heart and the drop of my stomach. I turned from his deep-brown eyes and noticed the two plates on the counter next to a large box.

"Vito's?"

"Yup." He strolled over to the fridge and retrieved two bottles, then popped the tops off. "Still the best pizza in town."

"Man, I've missed that place."

Not only was it the most authentic pizza I'd ever eaten, but the stories Fedele Vito would regale us with from the "old country" is how we'd spent many a Friday night after football games. Memories of sitting squished in a booth, next to Marcel, with Regina, Irene and others came flooding back. Especially the way he'd let his thumb stroke the base of my neck, or how I'd need to hold his hand. We'd always had to touch in some way or another.

I let my fingers brush against his when I took the offered beverage. I craved the constant physical connection we'd once had. It made zero sense that being around him again created so many emotions. But if I were honest, the possibility had played into my avoidance of him. There were times I'd thought about what I'd say or do if I were ever to come face-to-face with Marcel again. I'd worried how he'd react to seeing me. I didn't regret much in my life, but the way I'd left things with Marcel was one. Probably the biggest one.

Being back, I had my answer. There was tension between us. Hurt. But we also still had our connection. The one that made anything seem possible.

He stepped closer and kept his gaze locked on mine as he took a drink. I could only watch and wish the lips wrapped around that bottle were on me instead.

I put a hand on his chest, torn between pushing him away or crumbling up his pristine shirt by yanking him down.

"What else have you missed, Cyn?" His voice dropped and took on that extra huskiness which had always caused my heart rate to spike, all moisture to leave my mouth, and a familiar tingling to pulse between my legs.

Nothing had changed as I shifted my weight from side to side, trying to work it out. I'd missed so much. Especially in the beginning. Him. Us. How good we were before...but I couldn't say any of those things. To do so would be admitting I was...not wrong, hasty maybe, but not wrong in my choice. That I stood by. But how I handled it, and that I'd hurt him...hurt him more than I let myself believe I could.

Instead of speaking, I set my bottle down as he took another drink from his. I ran my hands across his chest, feeling the muscles beneath. He didn't stop me. When I lifted the hem of his shirt to slip my hands under, still he didn't stop me. Memories danced on my fingertips. So many years had passed, but at the same time, touching him like this was as natural as ever.

Our first time, as cliché as it was, happened on prom night. At the edge of my aunt's property, under the stars in the bed of his father's restored 1950's pick-up truck. We'd planned the night. Marcel had tried to make it as romantic as possible with blankets, pillows, and candles. And he'd succeeded.

My actions were as tentative now as they'd been then. The heat of his skin warmed my palms as I ran them across his taut stomach. He tried to seem unaffected, but I noticed the tighter grip on his bottle and the slight balling of his fist as he attempted to restrain himself.

I licked my lips and stretched up on my toes to reach his neck. I inhaled before placing a tiny kiss on his collarbone. Somewhere in the back of my mind I knew this was probably a bad idea. Too much between us to muddy already dirty waters with sex. But being so close and being around him for the last few weeks, it almost erased the last two decades. It was like we were picking up where we'd left off.

Almost.

"Aren't you hungry?"

I looked up at him and smiled. "Very."

10

MARCEL

THIS WAS NOT HOW I IMAGINED THE EVENING GOING, BUT AS Cyn ran her hands up my chest and then down again, letting her nails scrape ever so lightly, I was not going to complain. I set my beer down and cupped her face. Since the morning I'd seen her I'd wanted to kiss her.

She tilted her head up, her lips parted, and I let go of my threadbare restraint. Cyn wrapped her arms around to grip my back as I plunged my tongue into her mouth. The connection and remembrance was instant. The years melted away and I was transported back to the first time I'd ever gotten this pleasure. She no longer tasted of watermelon Bubblicious. The sugary sweetness replaced with a subtle mint and a hint of vanilla. My heart raced as much now as it had back then.

Soft lips and barely audible moans. Still as good as I remembered, if not better. Our tongues danced, her fingers dug into my flesh, and it was the perfect mix of pain with the pleasure. My dick hardened, and I pushed my hips forward. She needed to know the effect she had on me, even after all these years.

The evidence of my erection didn't make her stop. Instead, she slipped a hand between our bodies and gripped it through the fabric. I broke from the kiss and let out a low groan. This wasn't enough. I needed more. I needed to get lost in her if only for a night. I rested my head against her forehead. Both of our chests rose and fell in deep, exaggerated breaths.

She kept stroking me, and I was liable to lose my shit early before things really got started.

"Is this what you want?" I croaked out.

She stepped away. The absence of her hands on my body was a stark change, and I didn't like the emptiness. She moved over to her purse...shit, was she leaving? She pulled out something gold and turned back with a wide grin as she let her treasure dangle from her fingers.

"You can thank Regina."

I grabbed the foil packets and wrapped my arm around her waist, taking the opportunity to kiss her again. Keeping her close to me, we headed down the hall to my bedroom. I'd thought about taking her in the kitchen, but for what I had planned, we needed comfort. I had years of lost time to make up for, and I was going to try my damnedest to do it all in one night. True, we had things between us that needed to be aired out, and one night of passion wouldn't change that fact. There was a talk to be had.

In the morning.

I tossed the condoms onto my king-sized bed before turning my attention back to the beautiful woman standing in my room. The woman who had on entirely too many clothes. Stepping closer, I ran a finger down her chin, trailing a line down the front of her neck until I got to the button right above her cleavage. She started to undo it when I stopped her.

"That pleasure is going to be all mine. The best part of a gift is unwrapping it."

She rolled her tongue along her bottom lip. "Is that so?"

I nodded and undid the first button.

She glanced down. "And do I also get to do some unwrapping?" Her gaze lingered on the obvious imprint in my shorts.

I shook my head. "Tonight we play by my rules."

She tilted her head to the side. "You have rules now?"

I undid another button while nodding again. "Some things change."

In slow motion, Cynthia spread her arms out to the side and let her head fall back. "And somethings stay the same," she whispered.

Unable to resist, I bent to kiss the exposed skin of her neck and made quick work of the remaining obstacles.

The fabric parted, revealing the prize beneath. Smooth brown skin and large breasts hidden behind a black lace bra. My breath hitched. Regardless of how much I wanted her naked, I was not going to rush this.

Starting with my thumbs, I brushed along her collarbone, letting each finger join in one by one. Sliding across her soft flesh until I pushed the shirt off her shoulders, down her arms, and onto the floor. Keeping full contact with her skin, imprinting the feel of it on my fingertips.

"Am I allowed a kiss?"

I didn't answer her question. Instead, I pressed my lips against the small space behind her ear that'd teased me this morning. Then down the side of her neck, running my nose along it, getting drunk on the sweet rose scent. Hands on her waist, I walked us backward until her legs hit the bed.

I licked down the front of her neck, circling the small divot at the base with my tongue.

My fingers itched to cup her breast, and my mouth watered at the promise of worshipping them, but all in due time.

"Cel, please," she moaned.

I smiled at her before slowly kneeling, peppering kisses as I went. A small tattoo of a bird flying free of its cage with the words "Let it go" took me by surprise.

I ran my thumb across the ink. A tattoo was the last thing I expected to see. The design and location near her hip bone told me what it was for and seeing it was ice water. I'd never tried to keep her from her dreams. I'd supported her, understood why, and still she'd left. I closed my eyes and pressed my lips to it before standing.

"Marcel..."

I could only shake my head before I walked out of the room. I took in slow, controlled breaths as I pulled another beer from the fridge and drank half of it down in one gulp.

She paused at the entrance of the kitchen. "Should I go?"

I glanced at the untouched pizza. My appetite disintegrated much like my libido. "You should eat first."

"Always taking care of me," she whispered.

"Old habits die hard."

There was so much I wanted to say, but I didn't trust myself to let any of those words free. Instead, I remained next to the fridge as she pulled a slice from the box. Cynthia sat and ate in silence. She'd been the one who'd left, yet I'd been the one who'd felt somehow in the wrong. Like my feelings weren't valid given the situation. And they weren't. Not then when she'd fled without as much as a goodbye. And not now with no apology or real explanation being given.

"What time will you get started tomorrow?"

I briefly glanced at her, then finished my beer. The flavor could have been chalk for all I cared. I didn't taste anything and had to force the swallow down past the lump in my throat.

"Probably eight or so if that's good. We can start earlier since you don't have any neighbors and aren't living there."

I turned, gripped the edge of the apron-front sink, and stared out the window. Six years. Plans to take on the world together. Six years dismissed in two pages. My love for her a burden, holding her back from living the life she'd wanted. It was only teenage love that wasn't meant to last. That part hurt more than the rest. Everything we'd shared, everything we'd felt, she'd written off. As if I couldn't be sure of what I'd wanted then. Of who I'd wanted. Age made no difference in those feelings. Having her back after being gone for so long proved that.

I didn't turn when I heard the scrape of her chair or the

sound of her footsteps. She placed her hand on my arm, and still I refused to look at her. I couldn't.

"Cel, I..."

I stepped away. "It's late, and I need to get an early start tomorrow." I lifted my chin in the direction of the pizza. "Take it with you."

"I guess I'll see you tomorrow."

I crossed my arms, needing to put up some sort of barrier. Work. This was a job, and I needed to stay within those bounds. "You don't need to be there every day."

"Is that your way of saying I shouldn't come?"

I clenched my fingers. "Should be easy, right? Staying away." It was an asshole statement, and the deep frown on her face let me know she thought the same.

She snatched her purse from the chair and opened her mouth to speak but closed it again. With a heavy breath, she shook her head and started out of the kitchen. "Night, Marcel."

My need to fix it, to talk things through, battled with the frustration and fresh pain from the old wound being ripped open. She waited, almost as if she'd hoped I would say or do something. When I didn't, she left without another word.

CYNTHIA

I laid in bed staring up at the ceiling. Regina being asleep when I'd returned last night had been a welcomed reprieve. I hadn't been in the mood to be interrogated, and still wasn't. Hurried footsteps down the hall, followed by her muffled voice as she spoke quickly to someone on the phone. More rushing down the hall and back again, followed by the slam of the door.

I glanced over at the clock. Six a.m. I was tired but couldn't sleep. All night I'd tossed and turned, haunted by the look on Marcel's face. I hadn't thought about the tattoo, it'd been a part of me for so long. And even if I had, how would I bring it up without talking about the thing I wanted to avoid. The decision had been made, the deed done. Rehashing it with the other possibilities that could have been done differently didn't do anyone any good. Didn't do *me* any good.

Besides, I'd explained it all to him. What more was there to say? What we'd had was simply a teenage infatuation. At least that's what I'd told him. Happily married childhood sweethearts weren't a thing. Not in my experience anyway. We wouldn't have lasted because he wanted a type of life I didn't. I slipped my hand under the cover and lightly ran my fingers over the area on my stomach, closing my eyes as I remembered the decision to get it. It served as a reminder that I'd made my choices. Leaving him may have been hard and painful, but it'd needed to be done.

Marcel may have believed I'd walked away and never thought twice about him again, but he was wrong. He was foremost in my mind when I decided to get inked with some of my college girlfriends. An impulse when my heart ached from missing his birthday for the first time. I didn't trust myself to call him and had repeated the mantra I'd adopted to get through the worst of it: the clean break was for the best. For him and for me. No amount of love and respect could overcome two fundamentally different wants in life. I'd loved him enough to let him go.

When my friends had asked the meaning, I'd lied to them and said it was a special saying between my aunt and me. My choice was mine. And private. And that choice, like the one to leave this town, had shaped who I'd become. For better or worse, I was who I was, and I wasn't willing to change that or apologize to anyone for it. Including the man I'd hurt in the process.

And he was hurt. The sadness in his eyes. The slump of his shoulders. Marcel had a great family life. His parents provided positive examples of what a healthy marriage should be. And it had been something I'd always known he'd wanted. And something that had always scared me. For all the love I'd had for him, the years we'd had together...I'd remained scared. Becoming like my parents—more importantly like my mother—was my biggest fear and driving force. She would have loved to know I'd ended up in her same predicament. She would have seen it as karma since my existence "ruined her life" and derailed all her grand plans.

Absentmindedly, I stroked the delicate necklace, pressing my thumb into the small diamond in the center of the cross. "Don't be scared" were the words Auntie Drea had said to me the day I'd sat at the table worried she'd be so disappointed in me. She'd been the only adult I'd confided in, and she'd kept it between us with no judgment and no disappointment.

Marcel hadn't judged me, either, but much like his reaction to the tattoo, he'd been hurt, even if he wouldn't say it out loud. But now...now he was getting a chance to say all the things I'd denied him.

"That should be easy for you. Staying away." I curled into a ball, remembering the bite in those words. Not as easy as he believed.

⚜

SECOND THOUGHTS SWIRLED in my mind as rapid and murky as the cloud of dust from the gravel road. He'd pretty much told me not to come, but it was my place. He didn't have to take the job, but he did. He worked for me, and I could be onsite. Marcel was angry and he had a right to be, but we were adults and could act as such.

The crunch of my tires and light squeal of my brakes made the guys throwing debris in the large dumpster look over then wave their greeting. Several trucks were parked at angles on the grass. All but the one I came to a stop behind. Marcel's sat in the middle of the driveway, the Lewis Construction emblem mocking me and making me second guess my actions. Showing up despite his unspoken request not too was my hardheaded decision. *Too late to chicken out now.* Grabbing my water bottle, mask, and gloves, I paused for a moment then exited my car.

This business was going to be mine. It *was* mine. The new beginning I needed. The one I wanted. The decision to return home, to return to my roots hadn't been one I'd made lightly. But it had been made and I wasn't running from it or backing down from putting my all into succeeding.

Being a part of the renovation was important to me. It was a step necessary to solidify the path was the correct one. The history between Marcel and I would not overshadow that. I wouldn't allow it. Living my life as I saw fit for the last two decades would not suddenly change, unlike my location.

MJ stood on the porch with Jerry and stopped talking mid-sentence on my approach. "Good morning, Ms. Cynthia. I didn't think we'd be seeing you today."

I'm sure he didn't, depending on what his father told him. "Changed my mind about coming. Your dad inside?"

"Yes, ma'am. Up on the third trying to figure out a plan. But...well, I'll let him tell you."

Shit, that couldn't be good. I knew there was an issue with trying to add what I wanted, but it was important to have an owner's suite on the property. A few of the crew that I walked by all greeted me on my journey up the steps. I couldn't help but glance at the closed door on the second floor. A blaring reminder I needed to make a decision about that as well.

Marcel stood at the top of the landing, alternating between looking at the blueprints in his hands and appraising the attic space. The intense focus of him trying to take care of something for me brought back more memories. He was always attempting to problem solve, make things work. To make me happy. The warmth of that knowledge warred with the memories from last night, and of the teensy bit of guilt in my decision to not give him the space he'd asked for.

"Good morning," I said, locking those worries in a box to focus on the task at hand.

The oppressive heat of the uncooled space should have quickly turned arctic from the immediate change of his body language. He dropped his head, his posture went rigid, and the deep, audible inhale he took could have sucked all the oxygen out of the room.

He rolled up the blueprints, tapping them against his thigh twice before turning to face me. "Morning."

No warmth in his eyes. No smile on his face. Neutral indifference with a side dish of annoyance.

Nausea and uncertainty rolled my stomach. "I know what you said, but this is mine and..."

He waved me off with the papers in his hand. "You want to

be here, fine, be here. I had to call you later anyway. This." He spread his arms around turning from side to side "Can't be done without some additional major overhauls. It might actually come out cheaper to build you a free-standing structure on the property."

"What?"

"This, what you want, the systems aren't made to handle that much of an extra load."

At least his frustration had shifted gears to something other than me. Or maybe it was wishful thinking on my part. He went on and on about subflooring not having the proper support and the cost of beefing that up, with issues then moving from the plumbing to the electrical to the heating and air systems. I didn't understand everything he talked about, but the gist was a shit ton more work with even more money than we had in the contingency fund to cover.

"I can build you a tiny house adjacent for less. I mean you'd still go over budget, but not as much. Or..."

The deflation from the bad news had me more on edge than I'd already been. Though as he explained everything, the hostility seemed to disappear. He was completely in his element when it came to his work. Pride rolled off him when he spoke. A new side of him since carpentry and construction hadn't been his interest before. *"You knew me..."* The little comment he'd made on the phone popped back into my head.

"Or what?"

He rubbed the back of his neck. "You could move into your aunt's room. The plan, if you turned it into a guest suite, was to break down the wall to the bathroom on that level anyway. You wouldn't have a kitchen, but it's plenty big for a sitting area."

Once again, I gripped the necklace. Over the years, the thin, precious metal had become my talisman of sorts. Why did it feel like I was doing something wrong to take over her space? But at the same time, I couldn't leave it as some sort of unplanned shrine, either.

"You don't have to decide today. I...I know it's a lot." And just like that, the warmth and caring was back in his voice. Like the tension between us had been put on pause so he could give me the emotional support he knew I needed in that moment.

I swallowed the dryness in my mouth and looked up at him. He moved closer but stopped just shy of reaching me. So many times, his arms had been my security. Their strong embrace hugging away the pain and communicating that everything would be okay without the necessity for words. Those days had long passed. And after last night, I didn't think they'd be returning.

I'd lived. Taken care of myself. Not to mention had a team of people who'd looked to me for decisions. The buck had stopped with me and I'd handled it all. There was no reason I had to all of a sudden revert back to needing outside support simply because he was here.

"No to moving into her room. From a business perspective having three guest suites would be better than two. Do you know the cost difference between the attic and the tiny house option?" I ignored the pit that dropped in my stomach, but I knew her room couldn't remain untouched.

He glanced around the hot attic, wiping sweat from his head with the handkerchief from his back pocket. "No hard figures, but I'd hazard to guess it'd be about a six to seven grand difference. Give me a day to run the numbers and I can let you know for sure."

"Oof, that's a bigger difference than I expected. My only worry about a separate unit is having to walk from there to the main house in the rain. Or cold," I added with a small laugh.

"We do our best with the initial estimates, but sadly something always comes up in construction."

For the moment we talked like two people without tension between us. Simply client to contractor discussing the scope of work to deal with. But it was blown to hell when a tingle shot down my spine as he placed his hand on my lower back to guide me from the space. The contact made me want to grab his shirt and kiss him in hopes the act would say all the words I couldn't seem to speak.

Being confronted with his pain over my abandonment left me confused. The lies I'd told myself had been obliterated. I'm sorry. Two simple words were now the hardest thing for me to say because they came with a "but," and the truth that came after...it would do more harm. I'd been running from that since the day I'd left.

For a half a second, time appeared to stop as if we battled with the same thought. A slow blink broke the spell. "We can figure out the best location, maybe some sort of covered walkway. Though you don't want to change the look of the main structure too much. Either way I'll give you the options and we'll move forward with whatever your choice is."

The thought of living in a house Marcel built warmed me in unexpected ways. The fact he would make it sturdy and secure. A house that would no doubt stand the test of time. Like his apparent love for me.

And mine for him.

Despite all the hurt between us. Mostly from me to him.

He was a good man. And I was glad he'd found happiness with someone and suddenly wanted to know more about the Ex-Mrs. Lewis. She'd given him what I wouldn't. At the bottom of the landing, he pulled his hand away, but we stood close. The same wounded look of longing appeared in his beautiful dark eyes, and it stabbed at the part of my heart I was sure I'd shut down for good. It'd been in hibernation for years, but like a bear coming out for the spring, it was hungry. And there was only one way to feed it. Only one man that could sate that appetite.

I reached up to stroke his face, and he didn't recoil from my touch. He'd done so much for me when we were together. He'd deserved better than how I'd left. I swallowed the dryness in my throat.

"Marcel..."

"Hey, Dad. Oh sorry."

We both turned to see MJ standing there, eyes wide and brows raised damn near to his hairline.

My moment of courage dissipated. "I'll let you work." I gave his son a quick glance before heading down the stairs and out the front door. The wide-open space was my only hope to get enough air into my constricted lungs.

❧ 12 ❧

MARCEL

"Okay, kids, gloves and hardhats on. Twelve and under, you are only picking up the debris and trash. You'll be with Harold. The rest of you, get with your buddy and watch, listen, and learn."

The ten members of my woodworking class did as instructed and peeled off to their respective areas. Classroom settings could only teach so much, so it was nice that my clients usually agreed to let them attend at least one live day on a jobsite. Sometimes more depending on what was being done. When I'd mentioned it, Cynthia hadn't hesitated in her agreement, and she'd even gone so far as to commend me on what I did to share my skills and knowledge.

Her praise felt good, and she'd even said she looked forward to seeing the kids in action. But that was before the tension between us had skyrocketed. She'd not been around the jobsite for a couple of days and had given me what I'd wanted. Or thought I wanted. Space. Space to get my head on straight and to get my bearings back. Not like her presence mattered much; simply being at this house brought back all the thoughts. If she didn't show, I would need to call her. We needed an answer sooner rather than later about the third floor.

Pushing the wayward thoughts away, I began taking notes of the rotten corbels on the porch. An hour into it, a cloud of dust got my attention. Despite my conflicted emotions about her staying home, a smile pulled at my lips with the possibility of seeing her. It quickly faded when the car that came to a stop was a dark-blue Honda Pilot instead of the gray Toyota.

Cussing under my breath, I put on my most pleasant face and went to greet my sister. I'd been dodging her calls, so I knew it'd only be a matter of time before she tracked me down.

"By and by, you are alive. Imagine that." Jennifer slammed her door shut with her hip and I jogged over to help with the trays she had in her hands.

"You know I am. I'm sure your blabbermouth husband is the reason you're here." I leaned down to kiss her cheek, getting a side-eye and half smile in return.

"Well, if you'd answered your damn phone when I called, he wouldn't need to tell me what I need to know. You make me resort to blackmail."

She strolled around to the back of her SUV, popped the trunk, and pulled a folding table free. She always knew which days I had the kids at the job since the program had to be approved by the outreach board—which Eddie was a member of —I had to send them a request each time I wanted the kids at a location. Even in a small town where everyone knew everyone, red tape still needed to be cut, permission slips and waivers of liability signed. Jennifer did her best to bring lunch for the kids and crew on those days.

"So..." She made quick work of setting up the table before grabbing the tin containers back from me.

Yup, the way she dragged out that word and her constant looking around as if she were searching for someone meant the interrogation was coming.

"She's not here, so you can stop looking."

"I don't know what you're talking about." Her voice went up an octave, a clear indication of her shoveling bullshit.

"Right. I'm sure you don't. Look, I get it you want to be nosey, but I cannot and will not get into this with you here."

"Well, if you'd answered the damn phone we could have already talked."

I loved my sister, I really did, but lord, the woman never seemed to understand I had a mother. The very same one we shared. That fact didn't stop her from meddling in my business and trying to run my life. I was pretty sure she was the reason both my kids had taken an extra interest in my love life.

"There is nothing to talk about," I called over my shoulder, going back to her car for the paper products that were left behind.

"Like hell there isn't, Marcel John Lewis."

"Really, Jennifer Marie King."

She pursed her lips, narrowed her eyes, and snatched the plates from my hand. "You not gon' tell me there is nothing to talk about when the very woman you were all broke up over has returned and you here fixin' her house."

Arguing with her was pointless. Years of experience had taught me that. Headstrong and stubborn were the two best words to describe my sister. Well, the two nicest ones at least. I knew she meant well, but at forty-four, I did not need her trying to make things better.

"How about I come over Sunday. I'll let you feed me and once I'm good and full, you can play detective."

She crossed her arms and leaned back, looking me up and down. "You'll 'let' me feed you. Wow, however did I get so damned lucky?"

I wrapped my arm around her shoulders and squeezed. "Some folks just end up with all the luck, I suppose."

The back of her hand connected with my chest and I spun away, laughing.

Lunch came and went with no sign of Cynthia. By the time we were wrapping up, I didn't want to admit another day of not seeing her made for a bit of a disappointment. And brought up the old wounds I'd thought were long since healed. She was avoiding me. Again. Though this time at my request. I couldn't be mad at her for doing what I'd asked.

With the crew gone, I took time to sit on the back porch and take in the property. Quiet and peaceful. It was a beautiful location; I'd always thought so. From the mossy oaks scattered around the acreage and lining the drive, to the weeping willows that surrounded the bank near the marsh, I could understand the appeal of living here, even if I'd always worried about Ms. Drea being all alone and removed from town.

But folks looked out for others here. It was one of the things I loved about my community. I leaned back, resting on my elbows as I stared up at the pink-tinged sky. The sunsets had always been more amazing out here. The dock Cynthia wanted built would be a spectacular place to lay back and enjoy them.

The slam of a door snapped my attention. Pushing off the porch, I dusted my hands on my jeans, expecting to see one of the crew as I rounded the corner. Instead, I found Cynthia.

She stood beside my truck with an almost guilty expression. "Sorry. I figured everyone would have been gone by now."

"It's your house, no need to apologize for being here."

The song of the cicadas played around us, accompanied by the occasional croak of a frog.

"Right, I just wanted to take a peek at what's gotten done the last few days."

Neutral. Work. I needed to find a way to treat this—her— like any other job. Even if I knew there wasn't a chance in hell of that happening. I waved her up onto the porch. "There's not a whole lot to see. We got started on some framing, stripped out the electrical, drew out placement for the new plumbing." I spoke as we climbed the stairs.

Her sharp intake of breath made me turn to face her. The second floor was completely open with next to no walls other than her aunt's room. The other thing we continued to work around. She'd said she was okay with converting it yet made no moves to clear it out so we could move forward.

"Looks a lot different, I know."

Slowly, she walked forward, letting her fingers gently touch the old stud before gliding over to the newer one. "Everything is just...gone."

"It can be a lot to take in."

"Right. Yes. Like, I know this is what needs to happen. But at the same time, I... It just seems like I'm destroying her home, you know?"

She looked up at me, her light brown eyes shimmering with unshed tears. In normal circumstances I'd seen clients get emotional about the changes happening to their homes, so the tears weren't completely unusual. However, they hit differently with her. My familiar need to comfort Cynthia overrode my logical brain yelling at me to keep my distance and keep it professional.

She wrapped her arms around my waist and leaned into the embrace I offered.

"You probably think I'm being silly."

"Not at all. You're not the first person to cry after I've ripped out the walls of their house."

She laughed and wiped at the tears on her face. "You go around hugging all of them?"

I shook my head. "Nope, this service is reserved only for the VIP clients."

She leaned back and narrowed her eyes. "I'm a VIP client?"

"Without a doubt. The one and only."

She pulled away, and I did my best to school my features to hide the disappointment over the separation. What was it about her that had me contradicting myself at every turn?

"I don't mean to keep you. I'm sure you've had a long and tiring day tearing up my house." Her words came complete with a sad smile.

Walking away. Going home and leaving her to her business

would have been the smart thing to do. I needed a shower, dinner, and an ice-cold beer. But I also couldn't leave her here alone. Not with it getting dark and the house not completely secure. Small towns meant less crime, not zero crime. Or at least that's what I told myself as I followed behind her over to the closed bedroom door.

She ran her fingers along the dark, paneled wood. "I have boxes in the car. I figured it was time." Cynthia briefly glanced at me. "Regina was going to come, but I told her to stay and relax. Something's going on at the bakery and she was extra frayed when she got home."

"I can stay." The words popped out before I could stop them. Last time we were together, it felt as if she wanted to say something before MJ had interrupted us.

"I can't ask you to do that. You need to rest and unwind. Between the three of us, I'm the only one sitting around twiddling their thumbs all damn day."

"You're not asking, I'm offering. So, unless you are gonna shove me out of here, let me help you."

She laid her hand on my chest, and I closed my fingers around her wrist.

"Thanks, Cel."

With my other hand, I cupped her cheek. She smiled and leaned into my touch. When she looked up at me with those honey-brown eyes and mouth slightly open, I inhaled deeply, drinking in her scent. She rolled her tongue along her bottom lip and a half-second debate raged. Did I step closer and take another seductive trip down memory lane? Or did I keep my head about me? I swallowed the dryness in my mouth, stepped back, and cleared my throat.

"Um, so, boxes in the car? Is it unlocked?"

She nodded quickly. I turned on my heel and jogged down the steps before I went back on my decision to not kiss her.

❊ 13 ❊

CYNTHIA

THIS ROOM WAS THE LAST VESTIGE. WE WORKED IN SILENCE clearing out the remaining clothes in the closet and dresser. Along with the little knick-knacks, pictures, and other random items left behind. Two years I'd avoided this room, but just him being here, working in concert with me, made the process less painful than I'd anticipated.

I'm sure Auntie would have had plenty to say about my head-in-the-sand approach to dealing with everything. But I was taking the house she'd loved so much and fulfilling her dream for it. A dream I'd shared and encouraged. For the brief time I'd entertained staying in Madison, I would have ran it with her. She would have loved to see it finally being realized. It was a reason to celebrate, and I had to remember that.

The man helping me along the way just happened to be an added bonus. I sneaked peeks while he carefully took things out and folded them with military precision. He'd left. Ran away, had to get free of the island. Same as I had.

Because I had.

I'd spent way too much time lying to myself to ease the guilt. I'd refused to let myself believe that my leaving would have any

81

real important impact on his life. *But it had.* He'd been hurt. He was still hurting in a way.

I ran my hand along my lower stomach as the haunted look in his eyes popped back to the forefront of my mind. An apology. It seemed so simple, so easy, yet not. How would he look at me once I'd spoken my truth? I'd loved him with everything I'd had, but still not enough to give him what he wanted most. Even if he'd said he'd understood, part of me believed he'd hoped I would have changed my mind. Hoped I would have later regretted my actions. How would he look at me knowing that I didn't?

The screech of the tape snapped my attention back from its wandering.

"Tomorrow I'll get here early and have MJ help me break down the furniture. There should be enough space left in the storage pod."

I closed the drawer, pushed my worries back into the box, and turned to face him. "Sounds good. And thank you again for staying to help."

His stomach growled loudly, cutting off any response he was about to make.

He placed his hand on his abdomen and checked his watch. "Damn, sorry about that. I haven't eaten since lunch."

"What the hell, Marcel?" I pulled my phone from my back pocket, bringing the screen to life. It was nearing eight p.m.; we'd been working for almost two hours. "Why on earth are you over there starving yourself?"

He laughed hard and deep as he stacked two boxes on top of each other and lifted them with ease. "I hardly think eating dinner a couple hours late constitutes me starving myself." He started walking toward me and stopped when we were face-to-face. "But, if you want to make yourself feel better for my overtime, I won't turn down you buying me dinner." He winked and headed out the room with his load.

Dinner? Again? It didn't go so well last time, but…yeah dinner. It was the least I could do.

"So, what do you want?" I asked when he returned a few minutes later.

"Huh?"

"Dinner? I'm buying, you pick since, as you put it, you worked overtime and I'm trying to assuage my guilt for keeping you here."

His pearly whites stood out against his smooth, dark skin when his face split into a large and slightly dangerous grin.

"I don't know, Cyn. That sounds an awful lot like you're trying to ask me out on a date."

We were at a weird place. One minute it was awkward to even be in the same room together. The next it was almost like we were teenagers again and the last twenty-five years hadn't happened.

I rested my hip against the mattress and crossed my arms. "If I am, are you going to turn me down?"

Marcel stroked at his beard and his gaze traveled down my body slowly and back up again. "I'd be a foolish man to turn down a free meal and the sexy company that comes with it."

I rolled my eyes and turned my attention back to the final box. "I'm already going to feed you, no need at an attempt of flattery."

Suddenly, he was in my space. Fingers on my chin, he turned me to face him. "Have I ever lied to you?" His dark eyes were serious, and the intensity sent a thrill through me.

I shook my head and swallowed. "No, but as you've reminded me, I no longer know you the same way."

He licked his lips, and part of me hoped the moment we'd had earlier would return. I wanted his mouth on mine, his hands roaming my body…

"True, a lot has changed, but a lot has stayed the same."

He held my gaze, and the longer I stared into the depths of his chocolate eyes the more my body temperature began to rise.

I turned away and finished up with the last box. There were five more that needed to go down to my truck, and with the storage container nearly full I didn't even want to think about where I was going to keep them. Another decision I was dragging my feet on: what to do with her furniture. It couldn't sit in the rent-a-container forever. Some I knew I'd keep and put back in the house, but the rest, donating or selling, I wasn't sure, but I knew I couldn't hang on to all of it.

"We're done here. Let's get loaded up and then I'll feed you."

He stacked two boxes. "If I pass out from all this manual labor and lack of sustenance, will you give me mouth-to-mouth?"

Yeah, weird place indeed.

I shoved him toward the door. "I'm not answering that." I grabbed a box of my own and followed him out.

Once all of them were secured in my truck, I let out one last sigh before shutting the trunk. "Hopefully Regina won't mind more stuff in her garage."

"If she does, you can leave them at my place."

"That sounds like a ploy to get me back to your house."

He put his arm up, resting it on the top of my vehicle and once again invading my space. He was a damn magician because he'd worked all day, gotten hot and dirty yet somehow managed to not smell of sweat and general funk. Or I was simply willing to be nose blind to it.

"Do I need a ploy?" The tenor in his voice dropped and I involuntarily clenched in response.

I ran my tongue along the bottom of my teeth. "No. But I promised you dinner."

A half smile lifted the corner of his mouth. "And dessert?"

I knew that question had jack shit to do about food. Last time we'd attempted this, a glacier erected between us and not even the hot Georgia sun could have thawed the iciness. Or so I thought. It could all be just him flirting as a way to distract me, or it could be more. Whatever it was, I was willing to play along because I liked this side of us. I'd missed us. Our relationship had always been easy. And moments like these, when we slipped into the old, familiar patterns, it felt right. Like we could build a bridge over troubled waters.

I slid my arms around his waist. "Tell me what you want. I'll pick it up and meet you back at your house."

He reciprocated the move. "Nope. Something tells me I won't be eating...well, food that is."

It was a good thing he was holding on to me, otherwise that comment might have laid me out. He was right, a lot had changed, and his innuendos piqued my curiosity over just how much. Old Marcel had always been sweet in his flirting. Compliments and affirmations of how much he'd loved me and how much I'd meant to him. Those words had gotten my heart to flutter and other parts of my anatomy eager for attention.

New Marcel was more direct, and forward. His kiss had nearly made me implode with need. He'd been wonderful back then, but now...I really wanted a chance to compare how good other changes might be.

"So, how much is this going to cost me?"

"Lucky for you I'm a cheap date. Meet me at Remi's."

I frowned and racked my brain trying to think of what restaurant that was, but came up blank.

Marcel laughed as he took my hand and led me to the front of my truck. "You don't remember Remi? Tomboy who Irene gave hell to all the damn time."

The lightbulb went off. Remi Martin. Regina and I never understood what Irene had against that poor girl.

"Oh yeah... She has a restaurant?"

He opened the door for me. "Not exactly. Follow me over to Third and Sycamore. You're in for a treat."

I climbed in and he shut the door behind me. I didn't know where he was taking me, but his excitement stopped me from questioning him.

14

CYNTHIA

As I trailed behind Marcel my thoughts wandered. What the hell was he not telling me? I tried to recall what sort of businesses sat in that part of town and all I could recall was the Martin auto body shop, a gas station, and a pawn shop, plus a few other places. None of them were restaurants, but new businesses could have moved in.

I was even more confused when he turned into the parking lot—the full parking lot—of the auto body shop. I pulled up beside him, our cars parallel in the cramped space. Marcel was rubbing his hands together, all grins. The delicious scent of charred wood and smoked meat hit my senses.

"You are going to love it. Best barbeque in town."

"At the auto body? Is that even legal? Or healthy?"

I didn't want to think myself to be bougie, but on certain things I was. My dining experiences being one of those. Portland had been full of local, organic, and exquisite places to eat. Chowing down next to motor oil was going to be a stretch. However, when he wrapped his warm fingers around my hand, I realized I'd happily suffer through it—once—for him.

"So, about five, maybe six years ago, Remi's cousin came to stay with her. Man was shit fixing cars but played a mean hand of poker and was even meaner behind a grill. He started cooking for our weekly poker nights and it morphed into him building a little shack out back and turning it into the 'it' place for all things grilled."

Past the simple brick garage that sported Remi's family name was a smaller building that damn near looked like it was put together with scrap wood. The words carved into the door were simple: The Shack.

"The guys and I helped him put this together. I knew he didn't have a lot of cash, so we donated our labor, used leftover materials from other jobs. I seriously think we came out on top since we still get discounts on our food."

I glanced up at him, then back at the building. He'd helped a man that by all accounts he'd barely known. And not just him, but his crew. Another look at the place, and the haphazard design was on purpose. They wanted it to look a little rundown. None of his accomplishments had anything to do with me, but looking at The Shack, just like the retail spaces near the board-walk filled me with an odd sense of pride.

Inside, people called out his name once he stepped over the threshold. It was like he was Norm from *Cheers*. A few of his workers sat at tables, some together, others with whom I suspected were their families. They all politely acknowledged my presence.

After a few brief conversations, he led me to the simple counter. One end included bar seating and the other was where we placed our orders. A teenaged boy behind the register greeted us.

"What are you in the mood for?"

I looked up at him then at the menu hanging from the ceil-ing. "Pulled pork."

"Okay, pulled pork for her, and I'll take the Itis platter. Two beers."

Marcel had his wallet out and card in the kid's hand before I could even blink. "I thought I was buying dinner."

"You can get the next one."

"Next one?"

"Yeah."

At the end of the counter sat a woman that looked about our age. Blue, dirty coveralls covered her legs, but the top was tied around her waist revealing a white tank top. Her hair was cut low, like buzz cut, line-up low. On the other side, a man with a full beard, durag, and white apron stood talking to her. Marcel led us in their direction. Both people smiled when they saw us, but hers faltered when her gaze landed on me. Remi?

All things considered, I thought Remi would have been like me, trying to get out of Madison as quickly as possible. She'd battled so much shit from the rumor mill saying the reason most of her friends were male was because she'd slept with them all, to having to deal with new whispers once she'd revealed her sexuality. Irene had laid off for a while after that, which had surprised the hell out of me and Regina. Though I had to give it to Remi she gave it back to Irene just as good as she got, and she never let any of it bother her. At least, not that she'd showed. Marcel introduced me to the pair. The man was Al, proud owner of the place.

"Aren't you a blast from the past?" she stated. I wasn't sure whether to shake her hand or hug her. But she leaned in and gave me a quick embrace. "I heard you were back."

"Yup. Starting a new business. Or that's the plan anyway."

"Oh nice. So planning to stick around, huh?"

I glanced over at Marcel and nodded. "Yup. Guess a little piece of me always remained here, so it was time to come home."

The people seated next to her also knew Marcel and introduced themselves. I stood awkwardly by while the group of them chatted mostly about town stuff, some sports, all the while I fought the feelings of being an outsider for the first time.

Once our food arrived, we said our goodbyes. The place was packed so Marcel led us out to our cars. Other people in the parking lot were also sitting in or on their vehicles eating. He let down his tailgate, pushed a few of items out of the way before helping me hop up for a seat.

"You and Remi, I don't know why I never pictured you as friends."

He shrugged and opened his Styrofoam container. "She kept my old truck going much longer than it probably should have lasted. The woman knows her way around a car. I came in so much, the more we talked, the more we realized we had a lot in common."

It made sense. Marcel got along with most everybody. Even back in high school, though none of us were particularly close with Remi, there wasn't any animosity outside of whatever issues Irene seemed to have. Which Regina and I suspected mostly stemmed from the fact Remi didn't give two shits about most of what Irene seemed to think about her.

I turned my attention to my plate. I had to admit, it looked delicious. I went to take a bite but stopped, mesmerized by the sight beside me. Watching the man suck the chicken off the bone, I had to stop myself from moaning. His earlier alluded words about the oral he'd provide took up residence in the front of my mind. When he looked over, I quickly diverted my eyes. But not fast enough. His signature grin made its presence known.

As he slowly licked the sauce from his fingers.

"Want to try one?"

I wanted something alright, but it wasn't food. Still, I inched closer and grabbed a wing from the box. The messy sauce on the meat coated my fingers as I took a careful bite. Sweet, with a little bit of back heat, and fall-off-the-bone tender.

"Mmmm...not bad." I licked the sauce from my lips.

Marcel leaned forward and kissed the side of my mouth. His tongue softly lapped at the corner. He moved back before I could think to deepen the connection.

"I told you, best barbeque in town."

I'd never been much of an exhibitionist, but Marcel was

making me want to risk it all. My tongue darted out and licked at the spot he had.

"What's on the menu for dessert?" I asked, then took a bite of my sandwich, but not really tasting the flavor.

He cleaned another bone in damn near one swoop. "Hopefully you."

I guzzled my quickly warming beer. He went back to eating his food as if he didn't just set off a volcano of wanton desire. I needed to calm the hell down. Last thing I wanted was to make the town gossip by getting caught in a steamed-up car with Marcel. At least, not again. The memory of our first failed attempt at making out came flooding back and I laughed.

"What's so funny?"

I debated for a second or two. "Um, just thinking about when Old Man Johnson caught us on the edge of his property."

We'd wanted to go somewhere that was not the "usual" make-out space. Marcel nodded with a rueful look on his face as he cleaned his mouth and hands.

He nodded thoughtfully. "Ah yeah. Man, the lecture I got."

"Right. You got off easy. Granddaddy did like a month of sermons on the sins of premarital fornication and stared at me nearly the whole damn time."

That didn't count the grounding, or the lectures, or the talks of being just like my mother. The memory started to sour. Not that any of it mattered. We'd still found plenty of other times and places to be together.

"Believe me, I was getting those same looks. And your granddaddy came round offering 'counsel' to my parents." He took a drink of his beer. "You sittin' over there thinking about sullying my virtue on some dark country road? Because, I have to let you know, I'm okay with that." His pearly whites went on display before he took another pull from the bottle.

I couldn't help but laugh. "That's good to know." I leaned closer and whispered. "But can I sully your virtue in your king bed instead?"

"Yes, ma'am, you can."

I closed the lid on my half-eaten sandwich and hopped down off the tailgate. He did the same. The drive to his house seemed to be the longest ten minutes. I massaged my hip. We needed a conversation. The last time we tried this, things didn't end well. But he didn't seem to care or have a hesitation. We needed to talk, I knew this, but I was choosing to take the easy way and simply follow his lead.

No sooner than I'd killed the engine did he open my door. The moment I stepped out of my truck he pinned me against it. His mouth captured mine in a searing kiss. I parted my lips in surprise and he used that as an opportunity to sweep his tongue in. I gripped at his shirt. He grabbed my ass. Thankfully his back driveway didn't have a good view from the street, or we'd be giving his neighbors quite the show.

He ran his thumb across my bottom lip. "I've wanted to do that for days," he groaned.

"Maybe you shouldn't keep denying yourself things you want." My words came out in breathless pants.

He grabbed my hand and walked us into the house, pausing only to take off his boots and leave them by the backdoor. I did the same with my sandals. If I hadn't been so eager to get to his room I would have commented on the unlocked door. He didn't even bother to turn on the light. It didn't matter, I saw every-thing I needed clear as day. A soft glow filtered in through his sheer curtains from the streetlamp and bright full moon, bathing him in an almost ethereal light as he shrugged his shirt over his head and let it drop to the carpeted floor.

Touching him was a need I refused to fight. The muscles in his arms flexed when I ran my fingers over them, and he kept watch through hooded eyes. I leaned forward and flicked my tongue against his pebbled nipple. I was supposed to be the one on the menu, but as I moved over to the other side, I desper-ately wanted to taste every inch of this beautiful man. Wanted to express with my body all I failed to say with words. I kept laving his nipples and wandered my hands down his taut abdomen toward his crotch, moaning when I made contact with his erection. Every. Single. Inch.

Pulsating anticipation started between my legs. When I glanced up at him, I took my own advice. Holding either side of his face, I kissed him hard. With one hand around my waist and the other working to undo his pants, Marcel walked us backward toward his bed. The lust in his eyes was crystal clear when he pulled away. Tonight, he would not be stopping. That knowledge was like a release valve.

I pushed against his chest so he fell onto the bed. Grabbing the waistband of his pants, we worked in sync to get them off. His long, thick erection sprung free. My mouth watered. I kept my gaze on him as I lowered myself to my knees.

He leaned back on his elbows and grinned. "You know I'm the one expecting dessert."

Slowly, I wrapped my fingers around his stiff dick. It twitched in my hand. "Are you telling me no?" Down I stroked, then back up, circling the wide head with my thumb.

He shook his head. "Denying you? Couldn't do it back then, can't do it now."

"So, some things stay the same?" Again, I stroked his length, repeating my earlier caress.

He nodded.

Lifting up slightly, I wrapped my lips around the tip and sucked. Marcel fell back and grabbed at the blanket. Slowly, I lowered down, taking as much of him as I could into my mouth. His velvety skin was smooth against my tongue. Up again, and I licked around the salty head before drawing him in once more. When I cupped his balls, Marcel ground out a low, "Fuck."

Power surged through me at the primal sound. I released him with a soft pop and licked down his length. Once again, I enveloped him, hollowing out my cheeks. When he hit the back of my throat, I relaxed, exhaled through my nose, and took him deeper.

"Holy fuck!" He gripped the top of his head and propped his feet up on the bed frame. The action sent him down farther and I exhaled again to accommodate the intrusion.

I wanted this. I wanted him to fall apart at my doing. I eased up, his saliva-coated shaft moved in and out of my mouth effortlessly. With one hand I continued to massage his balls, with the other I stroked what wasn't in my mouth and bobbed my head faster.

"Cyn...baby...fuck. I'm about..."

I swallowed him again, just as his release shot forward and spilled down my throat. I kept sucking until his legs dangled free and his dick quit twitching. With a satisfied sense of pride flowing through me, I crawled up his body until I was on all fours above him. The spent look on his face, coupled with the lazy grin, sent zingers straight to my heart. There was no amount of lying I could do to make me believe I'd ever truly stopped loving this man.

15

MARCEL

CYNTHIA SQUEALED WHEN I FLIPPED US. ANY QUESTION OR protest was cut off when my mouth covered hers. I slipped my hand under her shirt, journeying north until I palmed her breast. The soft fabric of her bra didn't hide the hardened nipple that poked my hand. She moaned against my lips when I pinched it.

"You have on entirely too many clothes."

She tilted her head. "Last time I was here, you said something about rules."

Her coy expression faltered. Last time. I ran my nose down her jaw and over to her ear. There were things to discuss, but later. Tonight I wanted to experience her again. Without another word, I lifted the hem of her shirt. Cynthia raised her arms, allowing me to pull the barrier free. The light pink cotton bra that hid her glorious breasts was quickly discarded. Tossed to the floor with her top.

"Beautiful," I whispered. The weight of them felt like home in my hands. Soft and supple.

A light kiss to the column of her neck, then I trailed my tongue down to her cleavage, all the while committing the taste of her to memory. I lavished attention on one side, sucking and teasing one of her pebbled nipples while caressing and tweaking the other. Her moans were a siren's call.

Down her stomach with soft pecks, leaving a trail of goose-bumps on her flesh. The tattoo again gave me pause. I looked up at her as I ran my hand over the message.

She sank her teeth into her bottom lip and her warm hand covered mine. "I didn't just leave and forget about you, Cel. I never forgot about you, or us."

I kissed the design before continuing to undress her. More needed to be said. I wanted the explanation, to hear her reasoning. Her words were a temporary Band-Aid, but one I would take for now.

A patch of neatly trimmed dark curls greeted me as my treasure was revealed. I pressed my nose forward and inhaled. My dick twitched in response to her heady aroma. It was trying to come back to life as quickly as possible. I'd be ready by the time I'd sent her over the same cliffs of pleasure I'd enjoyed.

I pushed her knees apart and took in the view. Glistening perfection awaited me. Slowly, I ran my hands up her inner thighs. She sucked in a breath.

"Are you okay?"

Cynthia propped up onto her elbows, sexy smile firmly in place, sending another tug to my now semi-hard dick.

She widened her legs. "Bon appétit."

I licked my lips and inched my hands forward until I could run my thumbs along her tender flesh, coating the digits in her arousal. Keeping my eyes on her, I brought one to my mouth and sucked. Her chest rose and fell in exaggerated movements. She parted her lips, moistening the bottom one. I stared at her for another moment, a short window in which she could convey I needed to stop. When she didn't, I leaned forward and licked her slit from bottom to top. The delight of her on my taste buds made my eyes roll back.

I slid my hands under her plump ass and went to town. In rapid succession, I flicked my tongue across her clit, making her squirm beneath me. When I closed my lips around it and suckled the sensitive nub, she hissed and dug her fingers into my head.

I had a ladies first rule that she'd trampled. Making her pay in the form of multiple orgasms would be her just desserts. And I was going to take pleasure in giving her each and every one.

She started rocking her hips. "Oh yes!"

I dipped my chin, spread her pussy lips wide, and penetrated her as far as I could with my tongue.

Cynthia grabbed the comforter, bunching it around her head as she continued gyrating against my face. "Just...just a little more," she panted.

She used to contain her enjoyment behind muffled whimpers. I loved hearing her be vocal, asking for what she wanted. Her encouragement was fuel to the fire. Hooking two fingers, I inserted them, stroking her while continuing to lavish attention on her clit. She arched her back and let out a wailing moan. Her thighs seized around my head, and her inner walls quivered around my fingers. Once more I closed my lips on her sweet nub. Another gentle suck and she screamed out my name, pounding at the mattress.

Her arousal flooded my taste buds as I continued to tease her with my tongue while she rode out her orgasm. After a final swipe, I maneuvered over to my nightstand and pulled out the row of condoms she'd left. My attention went back to the beauty sprawled out still trying to regain her bearings. I licked my lips, tasting Cynthia. Her open legs were a beacon, inviting me in for another round.

The moment my mouth made contact she moaned and rolled her head from side to side.

"Oh god, Marcel."

I kept licking, moving up and down her aroused flesh. She arched again and released a long mewling noise. A primal need to see her come, to watch her lose all control at my doing took over. I sat back on my haunches and spread her sex. Making a V with my fingers, I rapidly stroked her slickened body with my other hand. The scent of her right under my nose. The light whimpers she made. And the sight of her rocking her hips made my now hardened dick weep in anticipation.

Her entire body quivered as her release took over. Mouth open. Eyes squeezed shut. And the death grip she had on my blanket was the reward I was chasing. Fuck, she was stunning in the throes of passion. I reached for the condom, fumbling with the foil packet before getting it open and rolled on.

My nirvana was in sight. I settled on top of her, my ever-eager dick poised at her entrance. I needed to kiss her, to be connected to her in every possible way. The moment I thrust my tongue into her mouth, she suckled it and wrapped her legs around my waist, hooking her ankles just below my ass. A gentle push had me smiling against her lips. Message received. Moving slow enough to torture us both, I inched forward, relishing in the movement. Once fully sheathed I stilled.

There was no rush. Cyn kissed my shoulder while her soft hands roamed my back, the feather-light touches a signal that this was indeed real. She was real. She was here. In and out. My pace leisurely as I made love to my first love again after twenty-five years. She placed her feet on the mattress and began moving in concert with my thrusts.

Damn, she felt good. The warmth of her welcoming body. The intermittent contractions of her inner walls. The soft sounds she made while she continued to caress my back. My heart squeezed.

Hot bursts of air hit my cheek as her breathing increased. I lifted so I could see her face; I needed to see her, to get lost in her eyes as she came undone with me inside her. Cynthia slid her arms under mine, gripping onto my shoulders as her body clenched around me.

I ran my hand up her side until I palmed her breast. Her nipple a hardened bud beneath my touch. Her body continued to pulsate, low moans rumbled in her throat as I slid in and out of her. Gripping her thigh, I flipped us so she was on top.

She smiled down at me, hair mussed, skin glowing. Fucking beautiful. She rested her hands on my chest, I used mine to squeeze and massage her breasts as she rode me. Confident. In control. Cynthia pumped her hips, gyrating on her way down, while managing to squeeze her walls around my dick. The move drew a long groan from me. She dropped forward and pressed her mouth to mine. Our tongues thrusting and swirling nearly in the same hedonistic fury of our bodies.

I couldn't resist smacking her ass. Her flesh hot in my hands.

"Fuck, Marcel..." Cynthia dug her fingers into my shoulders as her body shook and her thighs clamped against my waist.

My name pouring from her lips while she rode out another orgasm made my stomach clench. The tightening of her body pulled my own release to follow much sooner than I wanted.

Neither of us moved. The smell of sex lingered in the air, and her heavy breathing tickled my ear. I held her as the final shudders subsided and she finally rolled to the side.

"Are you okay?"

She placed her hand on her chest and laughed softly. "Never better."

After a quick kiss to her shoulder, I got up to dispose of the condom. It'd been one hell of a day and I was in need of a nice hot shower. I absentmindedly stared at the water. Being with Cyn was different, yet the same. Maybe better. Knowing I could still please her sent a wave of contentment through me.

"Mind if I join you?"

Her voice startled me. "No, not at all." I leaned in and turned on the second showerhead. "Get the temp adjusted to what you like." I left her and jogged down the hall to the guest bathroom, returning a few moments later. "Here you go."

She took the offered item, opening the small cardboard box and smiling. "How thoughtful." She popped the clear plastic cap onto her head.

"Whenever I travel, I also make sure to bring home these."

"Have a lot of ladies over, do we?" Her tone seemed playful, but the sharp look contradicted that.

Was she jealous? I had to work at keeping the grin off my face at that thought.

"No. A daughter who always seems to forget one. Also..."

When I bent down to pull out one of the spare toothbrushes she took advantage and grabbed my ass. I snapped a look over my shoulder and was met with a wink.

I set the plastic envelope on the granite counter. "A toothbrush and toothpaste. Extras from the dentist." I grabbed a washcloth and additional towel from the linen closet.

She eyed the package. "You have all the bases covered."

I shrugged and opened the glass door, allowing her in first. The large space seemed to shrink with her in it. She turned toward the water, letting it hit her face.

"You have an amazing bathroom. And I don't think I've ever seen so many body sprays."

I glanced above her head at the six units lining the wall. All placed at strategic pressure points.

"Face me."

Cynthia did as I asked without question. I reached around her to angle the top two downward then turned the diverter so they came on. She jumped from the surprise.

"I love what I do, but it's still hard on the body. After a long day, these things are like heaven."

She rolled her neck and sighed. "Hell yeah they are. I may need the name of the person that installed these so I can have them in my bathroom."

I picked up my bar of soap and worked up a lather. "Marcel Lewis."

She took in a sharp breath and frowned. "What?"

I ran my tongue along my teeth, tilted my head, and began rubbing my soaped-up hands across her chest in lieu of using the rag. I wanted to take any and every opportunity to have my hands on her.

"You wanted the name of the person who did the install." I drew circles around her nipples. "Baby, I'm in construction. I renovated this whole house after I purchased it."

She sighed as I moved down her stomach before grabbing the soap from the built-in niche. Slowly, she began running it across my wet chest. "I'm glad things worked out for you." She spoke keeping her eyes on her actions. "I mean that from the bottom of my heart." Finally, she looked up at me. "What you've done with your business. Your children. Even though I've only met MJ, I'm sure your daughter is just as wonderful."

She ran the bar of soap down my abdomen, stopping at my waist then back up again. The water rained down around us. I slid my hands down her hips, moving my fingers in small circles against her slick skin.

"I'm in awe, honestly. You seem to be leaving your stamp all over town. Like the restaurant tonight." Pride swam through me. She went back to running the soap over my chest. "I'm happy things...life, worked out for you. You deserve all the happiness and joy you've had."

There was a slight crack in her voice. The statement felt unfinished to me as she turned away to face the water. There was something more laced in her words. Sadness? Regret? I couldn't be sure. The unanswered lingering question of *why* prickled under the surface. I'd loved this woman with everything that I had, and in the end she'd said that love was holding her back. And the old, deep, cutting rejection, betrayal, and utter disbelief clawed for freedom. Now was not the time to let it out.

I stepped around so that I was in front of her. "I won't deny I've had a good life. I love my children, and had things been different they might not be here."

I wanted to say more. I wanted to add in how that didn't negate the fact her leaving hurt me in ways she would probably never know or understand. I wanted to say how her letter invalidated everything I'd thought we'd meant to each other. But I said none of those words.

It was an impossible place. To wonder what might have been if she'd stayed while battling the guilt over those thoughts knowing what, or better yet who wouldn't be here if that had happened.

❧ 16 ❧

CYNTHIA

DEAR GOD, THE MAN HAD LEARNED SOME TRICKS OVER THE years. Not that I had anyone to compare him to in our younger days, but Marcel had been an impressive lover even then. Time and age had made him a damn connoisseur. From the unhurried pace he set, to the gentle scrape of his calloused hands along my body, being with him was the same and yet oh-so-different.

"My, oh my, look who's doing the walk of shame this morning."

Regina's playful greeting pulled me from my daydream as I entered her house. I still couldn't believe I'd slept through him getting up, making breakfast, and leaving in the morning. The man had worn me out something good.

"Morning to you as well, Gina. Can I get a cup?" I asked, indicating to the coffee maker.

She set her travel mug down and filled a ceramic one for me.

"And there is no shame. I am a grown-ass woman. I walk back into the house wearing the same clothes as the night before with my head held high."

She tapped her mug against mine. "Amen to that. But you will have to tell me when I get home. Gotta go. Need to meet up with our accountant before heading to the bakery."

"Everything okay?"

She waved a hand as if to dismiss any worries. "Yeah, yeah. I'm sure it's nothing." Then she was gone in a blur of lime-green scrubs and red dreads.

My thoughts went back to Marcel. After our shower I'd wanted to leave, the mood between us had changed with us once again dancing around the topic neither of us seemed willing to bring up yet. But he'd convinced me to stay. Sleeping secured in his arms should not have felt as good as it had. Or as natural. Spending the night together wasn't something we'd ever been able to do. Stealing alone time had been hard enough, but we'd made it work. Too well.

I'd decided on the drive home, after the renovation work was completed, we'd sit and have that conversation. Put everything out on the table. *I'd* put everything out on the table once and for all.

If we could make it that long.

And that was a big if. But after was better to avoid a tension-filled working situation. A more tension-filled situation as we'd had our moments and undoubtedly would have more. But lying to myself was easier than admitting I wanted to avoid facing his hurt head-on for as long as possible. Getting a glimpse of it had almost been too much to bear.

Another worry wiggled to the forefront of my mind. As much as I'd told myself not to overanalyze what sex meant for us, I found myself doing just that. It could mean nothing, or it could mean everything. While I'd known Marcel would have been a factor to contend with—just like my family—the scenario I found myself in had never been on my radar. Mainly because I'd expected him to be unavailable. He was a good man who would move heaven and earth for the people he loved. But, just like my job being pulled out from under me, fate had saw fit to bring me full circle.

I pinched the bridge of my nose. "This is doing me no good," I muttered.

I was forty-three years old. I'd managed a brilliant marketing career, relationships, and life in general. I should have a handle on this sort of shit by now. Yet here I sat, trying to figure out what, if anything, spending the night with a man—that man —meant.

After checking my phone and replying to a text from my Portland friend, Sonya, I padded down the hall for a shower, rubbing the back of my now somewhat wavy hair. I needed a trim, and chances were Momma still worked at the only beauty parlor in town. Guess I'd be letting it grow out for the time being. I could only handle one fire at a time right now with Marcel getting all my attention. My reunion with my mother would have to wait.

❧

OVER THE LAST month I'd gotten used to seeing the same trucks parked around the house, so the new addition stood out. I grabbed my gloves and mask along with the box of pastries from my passenger seat. My now empty trunk space caught my attention as I climbed out. Marcel had managed to clear out the boxes before he'd left in the morning. He was always taking care of me. A slow smile spread across my face as his comeback replayed in my head.

The house was shaping up. The rotten boards of the porch had been replaced. Paint had been scraped, shutters were off to be repaired. Marcel and his team weren't wasting any time. My steps faltered for a moment, and I glanced up at the second story. Would they have already started tearing apart her room? I did a full body shake. It was time to look ahead at what I was creating instead of thinking in terms of what I lost or was losing.

"You're trying to start trouble." Marcel's voice boomed clear as I stepped onto the porch.

"It's lunch. How is that trouble?" a female voice I couldn't place refuted.

I exhaled nice and slow, stiffened my spine, and prepared to walk in on some argument.

"Morning." I attempted to sound light but wasn't sure if I pulled it off.

Both Marcel and his companion turned in my direction. The concert of hammers and saws faded away when the realization of who she was registered. With a dark complexion just as smooth and clear as his, and the same deep-brown eyes, his sister smiled, but Marcel appeared less than pleased with my arrival. I'd thought he'd left this morning to get an early start; maybe he left because he had morning-after regrets.

Her salt-and-pepper relaxed hair was pulled back and held in place with a satin headband that matched the gray scrubs she wore. "Cynthia." Jennifer approached with her arms wide.

I pushed the thought from my mind. "Good to see you. What are you doing here?" I asked, awkwardly returning her embrace.

"She's getting in my damn way."

Jennifer shot her brother a scolding look. "I stopped by to pick up my table and stuff I left yesterday. And I wanted to invite you to lunch Sunday. Or trying, but Mr. Grumpy wants to be an ever-present pain in my ass." She planted her fists on her wide hips and gave him another pointed stare.

"You're on my jobsite, interrupting *my* day. I'd say if anyone here is a pain in the ass it's you."

"Whatever. Look, I gotta run, my shift starts soon, but come over at one. Marcel will give you the address."

She waved and pushed passed me and was out the door before either of us could say no. Did I want to say no? I glanced at Marcel, who still wore a frown. Maybe I did.

"I'm sorry about her. Don't feel obligated just because she refuses to believe the only people that have to listen to her these days are her husband, children, and staff." He opened the lid to inspect what I'd brought.

"No problem. I don't want to encroach on your family time."

The mention of family made me once again think of mine. By now I was sure she knew I was back, and we were in a game of chicken to see who'd blink first. I'd resolved it wouldn't be me. Since spotting my mother at the bakery, I'd been extra vigilant when in town and so far had been able to avoid more sightings of her. I knew it wouldn't last forever, but I was hopeful she'd be in no rush to see me either.

He closed the lid and turned back to face me. "You aren't encroaching, I'm just trying to save you from an interrogation."

His statement bristled under my skin. "Interrogation? I don't think there's anything that I have to answer for."

My business with Marcel was just that—my business. I was too old to have someone—no matter how well-meaning or how close I used to be to them—trying to be in the middle of it.

He huffed a sardonic laugh and ran his hand down his face. "I'm sure you don't. Look if you want to come, come. I'll run as much interference as possible. If you don't, then don't. Either way I'll text you the address," he called over his shoulder on the way up the stairs.

My thoughts from earlier came back. Waiting until after this project was complete might no longer be an option. Even if the reconnection between Marcel and me was only that one time, we needed to clear the air if for no other reason than having to live in the same town again. But I couldn't let myself get sidetracked. Marcel was not the reason I'd returned no matter how great our night together had been. Eye on the prize. I had a business to get up and running.

I took one more glance up the stairs. Being here was not the best use of my time. Instead, I needed to focus on what I did best, start the marketing so I could hit the ground running once he completed the construction. And the separation of not seeing him every day wouldn't hurt.

"Leaving us already, Ms. Cynthia?" MJ called out as I headed to my truck.

"Yeah, I figure I should get out of the way so I don't slow you guys down any more than I already have."

He smiled, looking like his father when he did so, and strolled over to me. "We like having you around. The old man is a little less of a hard-ass when you're here."

He was a good kid, though at twenty-two not really a kid. Either way, seeing him was a flesh and blood validation that my decision all those years ago was the right one. A tiny validation, but I'd take it.

I reached out to pat his bicep. "I'll be sure to stop in so things ease up every now and then. But for today, there are pastries inside for you all. Hopefully, that'll make up for me leaving you guys with Mr. Hard Ass."

He barked a laugh. "That just might do it. Have a good day, Ms. Cynthia."

With a parting smile, I left my house and future in their capable hands.

❦ 17 ❦

MARCEL

I STARED UP AT MY CEILING, UNABLE TO SLEEP BUT NOT READY to get out of bed yet. Sunday was the one day we didn't work. Well, the day my crew didn't work. When a project was under-way, I seemed to always be on. Thinking of the next steps, making sure the materials were ordered, coordinating with the county inspections.

The fact that my brain couldn't shut off even though I wasn't working was the reason I was up at seven a.m. instead of sleeping in. That, and the nerves of having to sit through lunch with Jennifer and Cynthia. My sister thought she was slick, showing up at the site again like she had. I'd always dropped off her stuff after she'd provided lunch for the kids, she didn't have to come pick it up. I'd known the moment she'd pulled up what her game was. Jen had been pleasant enough, even gone so far as to hug Cyn and say how glad she was she was back, but I knew my sister. Something was up.

Cynthia and I hadn't even discussed our issues; I didn't want or need to try and hash that out with Ms. Nosy Pants acting as mediator. Or instigator. It could be hard to know which some days. I knew Jennifer meant well. I had been a bit of a mess back then, and she was forever the protector.

The vibrating of my phone cut through my musings. Porsha's number flashed on the screen. Her calling me first thing on a Sunday morning couldn't be good.

"Hello?"

"Hey, I didn't wake you, did I?"

"No, but a call this early can't be good."

The pause had me sitting up and preparing for the worse.

"Alicia was in a car accident last night."

"What? And you're just now calling me?" I tossed the covers back and headed to my closet. "Where is she? I can be there by eleven." I yanked a pair of jeans from the hanger and stabbed my legs in. I couldn't believe she didn't call me sooner.

"Slow your roll. This is why we didn't call last night. You overreact, get stressed, and generally go off the rails."

"Hell yeah I do. That's my baby girl." I put the phone on speaker and tossed it onto the bed so I could tug on a shirt.

"She's fine, Marcel. I promise. You know if it had been serious I would have called you sooner. But she's fine." Porsha's "calm" voice filled my room. I knew that tone. It was the one she took whenever she was trying to smooth something over or set me up for bad news.

Like when she'd wanted a divorce.

I dropped down onto the bed and picked up my cell. "Regardless, you should have called me when it happened. Especially since she's on my damn insurance." Now that the momentary panic had passed, I said a silent prayer for my soon to be higher premiums. "What happened?"

"She rear-ended a person. She claimed they stopped short but..." She didn't need to explain more.

I was surprised they hadn't suspended Alicia's license. If she'd not taken the defensive driving class—which clearly did zero good—the state might have. A dull ache formed in my head and I attempted to rub it away. This was not how I wanted to start my morning.

"I should make her drive the car all busted up for a while. Maybe that will teach her."

Porsha laughed. "She'd have a fit."

"Probably, but it would serve her right."

"Your call, but I'll let you tell her. She's still asleep. But really, Marcel, she's fine. I'm sorry for not calling last night, but she's really okay. Besides..."

My stomach sank. The way she let that word linger couldn't mean anything good. I shouldn't be dealing with so many issues before I'd had my first cup of coffee.

"What now?"

"Nothing. Nothing. Just MJ told me about your new girlfriend."

Fuck. Not that I needed to hide anything, but I knew better than to let my hands do too much roaming. However, girlfriend might be too strong a word. Cynthia and I were nowhere near a place that included labels.

"You been checking up on me?" I joked.

"Please. Our son calls me weekly to catch up. He told me about your new project." Again, she let the words linger.

Porsha knew about my history. I'd never forget the shock when she'd learned she was only the second woman I'd ever been with. So, if MJ told her about the house, Porsha knew exactly who my "girlfriend" was.

"Are you okay?"

Her question surprised me. I prided myself on our continued amicable relationship. I'd been stationed at Fort Benning and we'd met each other at a time when we both needed something from the other. Me to feel a connection to someone, to be wanted by someone. And she saw me being in the Army as a way out of Columbus and to see the world. We may have rushed into marriage and kids, but that didn't mean we didn't love, and more importantly respect, each other.

"Why wouldn't I be?"

"The woman that broke your heart is back. You know I'll

always love you, Marcel, and I want nothing more than for you to be happy. And not get hurt again."

I flopped back and closed my eyes. I knew she was coming from a good place but discussing any of this with my ex-wife did not sit well.

"I appreciate the concern. I do. But I'll be okay. I am okay."

She was quiet for a moment. "Alright. Just...be careful."

Again, I understood where she was coming from. And maybe I needed to be a little more cautious where Cynthia was concerned. However, at the same time, we weren't eighteen. So much in life had changed. We were different people. Older and wiser as the saying went.

"I will. And tell your daughter to call me when she gets up."

"Oh...she's my daughter now? A minute ago she was your baby girl."

"Yeah, that was before I knew the only thing really hurt was my insurance."

My day was completely off kilter after the phone call. New worries ran through my head as I waited for my coffee to brew. Had to call my insurance and wait to see if the person Alicia hit would claim injuries or not. I massaged my temples. I didn't need to deal with this on top of having to worry about what Jennifer would say at lunch.

I rolled the tension from my neck. Considering how Cynthia and I had left things two days ago, this meal could be worse than expected.

❧

I cussed under my breath at the sight of Cynthia's car already in the driveway. Hopefully, Jen would wait until after we'd eaten before she started in. Hell, I was still surprised Cynthia agreed to join us. I entered through the back door to find them seated at the kitchen island all smiles over iced tea while Cynthia chopped cucumbers for the salad.

"Sorry I'm late." I kissed my sister's cheek and handed her the bag of rolls she'd conveniently asked me to stop and get at the last minute. I walked around, hesitating before giving Cyn the same greeting. Jennifer watched me like a hawk. When I started to take a seat she was quick to tell me no.

"G'on in there with your brother, I'm almost done." She tried to shoo me toward the living room where I could hear Eddie yelling at the TV.

Instead, I headed over to the sink to wash my hands. "I can help. What else needs to be done?"

Over to the fridge she went. She pulled out a beer, used her apron to twist off the cap, and shoved it into my hands.

"I said out my kitchen."

Cynthia put her head down, but I could see the smile on her face before I walked out of the kitchen. That was a good sign, maybe. Some things never changed. My sister pushing me around, literally, was one of them.

"Afternoon, man," I said, dropping onto the couch next to him.

"She kick you out, too?"

"Yup. But for different reasons. I'm sure you were all in the way trying to taste test."

He laughed. "Hey, I'm only trying to help. What if it needed more salt?"

"Man, you and I both know you'd never tell her that."

He nodded. "You right. Anyway, so..."

"So..."

I craned my neck back over the sofa trying to see if I could hear anything. No luck.

"She's looking good after all these years. Like life's treated her well."

I took a pull of the ice cold, amber liquid. "Yup, she's lookin' good alright."

He twisted, appraising me up and down then smirked. "A'ight then."

"What?"

"Whatcha mean what? You know what."

I sucked my teeth and shook my head.

"Come on and eat," Jennifer called out.

Eddie grunted as he heaved himself up, his limp ever present on the walk from the sofa to the table. I glanced at Cynthia, trying to get a read on her mood. Her face was neutral with no hints of annoyance. Maybe my sister would not play the mother hen role today.

I whistled through my teeth. "Damn, Jennifer."

"What?"

"A simple lunch, huh?"

The spread laid out was more in line with dinner. Fried chicken, rolls, salad, and green beans. Hell, she'd even made a red velvet cake. Cynthia's favorite.

"It does look good, Jennifer," Cynthia stated. "You didn't need to go through all this trouble."

She waved us both off. "This ain't nothing big. And long as Eddie there don't overdo it, I won't have to cook tonight. I already set some aside for the kids when they get back from their friends."

Eddie rubbed his hands together and licked his lips. "Baby, I make no promises."

She shook her head and laughed. Eddie blessed the food, then we dug in. In the midst of the orchestra of utensils hitting plates and quiet chewing I snuck peeks at Cynthia, who sat across from me.

"So..." Jennifer started, and I let out a long exhale. "What? We not supposed to talk?" she challenged.

"Depends on what you plan on talking 'bout."

She put her elbows on the table and rested her chin on her linked fingers. "Simply tryin' to make conversation."

Cynthia looked at Jennifer then over to me. "It is what we're here for right? Some good food and catching up on lost time."

There seemed to be a distinct edge to her voice, though I wasn't sure if it was directed at me, or my sister.

"Ex-act-ly." Jennifer shot me a pointed look, and Eddie simply laughed and took another bite of chicken.

When my sister readjusted in her seat and stuck her chest out, I knew shit was coming. I sent my best warning in her direction. I wasn't playing games with her, and she needed to tread lightly.

She promptly rolled her eyes and focused her attention back on Cynthia. "Where you been hidin' and what brought you back? You just get homesick after all these years?"

Cynthia let her gaze linger on me for a moment, and a fleeting smile graced her lips before she shook her head.

"Not exactly. After college I ended up in Portland for a job. But after fifteen loyal years my company sold and merged with a bigger one and I was no longer needed. My position as marketing director was 'absorbed'." She made air quotes around the word.

"Sorry to hear that. People spend years giving their all to a place and get nothing in return," Eddie chimed in.

She took a drink of her tea and lifted one shoulder. "Yeah. I did get a nice severance package, so that helped. After I went through the stages of grief, so to speak, I had to figure out what was next."

I remained silent but was pissed on her behalf. The idea that they could treat someone...treat *her* that way after years of loyalty didn't sit right with me. At the same time, I didn't want to admit I was the tiniest bit happy she'd been fired since it had brought her home.

"Least with this thing you're doing now it'll be yours," Eddie said.

Cynthia nodded in agreement. I knew how nerve-racking starting up a business could be. The worries about if it would work or if it would be a failure. Being part of her new beginning, even if she hadn't planned on it, was special to me. I would do everything I could to help her succeed.

"This mean you replanting your roots?" Jennifer asked, but sent a pointed look in my direction.

I shook my head. A warning that she needed to not go down the road I felt she was headed.

A rueful smile pulled at Cynthia's lips. "Yeah, I guess you could say that."

"Hmph. Well, let's hope they stick this time. Because that man right there—"

"Jennifer," I snapped, cutting her off.

"What? Why you calling my name?"

"Because it needs to be said." I leveled my gaze at her and slowly shook my head.

She smacked her lips. "Fine."

Cynthia looked around the table. Eddie kept eating, knowing better than to get in the middle. Meanwhile, my sister and I were in a stare off. I appreciated Jennifer's concern, but I was forty-four, not eighteen. How I'd reacted then had not been my finest hour, but also not up for discussion in mixed company. Even if I was related to them.

❧ 18 ❧

CYNTHIA

"Okay ladies," I said, refilling my wine. "I know I'd always said I didn't want to hear about Marcel after I left but…I need to hear about Marcel."

Banning all talk surrounding him had been my coping mechanism. I'd supposedly been moving on with my life. That's what I'd told him. And that's what I'd made myself stick to. I'd been thankful both of them had abided by my request, Regina more since she was the only one of us to not leave for college.

"Uh-huh. But now that you done went and slept with him—"

"What?" Irene squealed through the phone. "When did this happen and why am I just now hearing about it?"

Regina bumped me out of the way with her hip so she could get front and center with the screen. "Oh yeah, chile. Came back on a walk of shame the other morning."

I rolled my eyes. "I told you there was no shame."

Irene's face got bigger when she moved closer to her phone. "How was it? He still the stuff dreams are made of?" She fluttered her eyes and cupped her hands under her cheeks before she and Regina burst out laughing.

Apparently neither of their asses forgot how much I may or may not have overly romanticized my time with Marcel.

"Can y'all just spill it?"

"Sounds like someone is trying to avoid answering the question," Irene said as she settled back against her sofa.

Regina eyed me up and down. "I think you might be right. I hope a man as fine as Marcel ain't a limp dick now and in need of the tiny blue pill." She took a sip of her chardonnay and watched me over the rim of her glass.

Being together always transported us back to our younger days. Gossiping, playful jabs, jokes, and so many laughs. Sure, I'd made friends in Portland, but none compared to the bond I shared with these two women. We'd gotten each other through some tough times.

"All I'll say is, I stayed overnight for a reason."

Their jubilant yells turned laughs filled the kitchen.

"Now, will you tell me something?"

They both exchanged some odd glances, much like Marcel and Jennifer had over lunch. There was something no one seemed to want to share. Because Marcel had certainly seemed to be trying to keep his sister from talking, and it wasn't just him attempting to run interference from her questions.

Irene answered first. "Well, I don't remember much since I left not long after you. I do recall him being moody."

"Pish, that's putting it mildly. That boy was pissed. I'd never seen him so...just, lost is the best way I can describe it. Kept asking if we knew, why didn't we stop you. Daddy damn near had to threaten to beat his ass if he kept coming around."

"Oh yeah," Irene chimed in. "Didn't he get in some trouble?"

Trouble? My Marcel? I drained the rest of my wine. He'd always been so level-headed.

Regina nodded, somewhat thoughtful like. "Yeah. To the point where I don't know how much joining up was his idea rather than his dad trying to save him from himself."

My mouth went dry and my stomach churned. My leaving had affected him that much? I couldn't believe it, but clearly there was something that happened, and guilt settled on me like a lead blanket.

"Did he say something? Why the interest now?" Irene inquired.

"Probably because Jennifer raked her over the coals today. She had lunch with them. Already joining back into the family fold." Regina answered for me as she got up to get a new bottle.

"Say what? Do I need to hop in my car to come defend my girl?"

I rolled my eyes at Irene. She was probably the prissiest of all of us but was also the first one talking about hold my earrings and ready to fight somebody.

"Slow your roll, Dr. Badass. I was not raked over the coals. She was asking questions about plans and things like that. It was more what wasn't said."

Regina refilled my glass and then her own. "Whatcha mean?"

"Well, much like you and Irene here just had some sort of silent communication going, Marcel and Jennifer did as well."

And now I knew why. Marcel didn't want me knowing how he reacted to my departure. If what Regina said was true, and he was that way with her and Irene, I could imagine he was possibly worse at home.

My old friend doubt came circling back around. I'd lived a good life, working, traveling, seeing the world. But had it been worth the hurt I'd caused? Had I been too selfish in my choice to leave? The questions made no difference now.

⁂

CONSTRUCTION of the third floor was underway. After too much time deliberating, I'd finally decided that staying in the house was what I wanted. It was what I needed. Though it had been tempting to live in a house Marcel would have built from the ground up, the conversion would be the next best thing.

While the crew worked inside, I sat on the back porch, out

of the way, thinking through my marketing ideas. I'd researched for months what sort of amenities a bed and breakfast should have other than the breakfast part. Luckily, I had that covered thanks to Regina. Nailing down a contract for her to supply the place with fresh bagels, muffins, and other pastries had been the easiest part of this process.

Some days I second guessed my decision. What the hell did I know about running a business, let alone one in the hospitality arena? But there was no going back now; giving this my all was the only option. There weren't many sights to see around Madison, so I needed to put my focus on the quaintness of the town. On slowing down and enjoying the small things in life as Marcel had reminded me when he'd voiced his opposition over the idea for a business center. People would come here for a change of pace and take a breath away from the hustle and bustle. For less crowded beaches and unique shops. We were different from Savannah or even Tybee Island as we were less known and more tucked away.

The serenity of Madison Island. Yeah, I could sell that.

The banging and constant on then off again buzz of saws in action played behind me. I'd tried to work on this at Regina's, but I needed to be here, to let everything this house, my house, and land had to offer seep into my soul and speak to me. This was where I'd always felt most at peace. And surprisingly, the noise helped me. It reminded me of my purpose, of my goal.

I picked up my notebook and stood. Maybe walking the property would give me some direction. Heading down toward the bank, I stood at the edge. A lot of people wouldn't think a marsh beautiful, but I did, and the platform would be a wonderful place for people to sit and relax. I turned to view the house from where I was, and an idea popped into my head. The area off to the right was open, flat, and a bit overgrown, but once I got landscapers out to tame the yard, it'd be a lush, grassy field. I'd thought about maybe having stables because I had the space and there were trails nearby, but that was an added headache I didn't need. At least not right now. Weddings, however, could be my moneymaker.

It'd crossed my mind before, but I'd put the idea of them on the backburner to focus instead on simply getting the place open. Setting myself up as a wedding location from the start could increase initial business. A thrill of excitement coursed through me as I walked toward my destination. It would be perfect for people who wanted picturesque weddings with a Savannah feel but without the premium price. I made a note to bring it up to Regina. I knew wedding cakes weren't her normal, but she was a baking aficionado. I was sure she could pull it off. Especially with Tricia's help, her being in culinary school and all. I started jotting down all the ideas.

"There you are." His voice boomed from behind and made me jump. Marcel ran his black handkerchief over his bald head as he approached.

I pressed my lips together to keep my mouth from gaping. The swagger in his gait, the way his shirt pulled across his chest as he moved. It was hot enough outside without him raising my body temperature by walking.

I closed my notebook, held it to my chest, and tried to temper my thoughts. "Did you need me?"

"I do indeed."

I knew his answer was directly related to my question and probably had something to do with the house, but I couldn't stop myself from thinking about my conversation with Regina and Irene last night. I took a steadying breath and forced my focus on the issue at hand.

"What are you doing out here?"

"Thinking this would be an amazing place for weddings."

He glanced around. The weeping willows off in the distance, the greenery that stretched on as far as you could see. Even the wildflowers that grew in a scattered yet almost uniform patterns. He nodded, and I could tell from his expression he saw the area the same as I did.

"It would be a beautiful spot to get married." He leveled his gaze at me, and I turned away from the weight of it.

"I'm going to need to track down some wedding planners that have new couples looking for locations still. See if I can coax them into touring and possibly booking here for a super discounted rate so I can have pictures for my website when I get it up and running."

I turned back to face him. "What's with that look?"

"What look?"

"That weird, dreamy look you have right now."

"Guess I'm in awe of watching genius in action in real time."

I rolled my eyes even though he couldn't see it through my shades. "Anyway. What did you need?"

"Oh, right. Have you made decisions on the finishes? I need to start ordering materials."

Shit. He'd given me samples last week and I hadn't even looked at them. "Um...when do you need to know?"

"Today would have been nice, but I'm guessing that is hoping for too much." He wiped at his head again. Only April, but the humidity was doing its best to kill us both.

"I'm sorry. Can you come over later? Everything you gave me is at Regina's. I'll cook."

A full megawatt smile spread across his face. "I'm never going to turn down free food."

"Great. And sorry for not having it sooner. I'm after perfection. The place has to have the right look and feel. But I also have been weighing the costs because it's a bigger factor thanks to the overages. What to splurge on opposed to what I can pick that's a little cheaper."

"You could have called or come over to the house."

"For what?"

"If you needed help trying to narrow down choices. Believe it or not, I do know a thing or two about all this stuff."

"You don't say." I feigned surprise. "Anyway, I have my picks mostly narrowed down. I know I want each room to have a theme and the selections should match."

"Guess you don't need me after all then." His commented sounded lighthearted, and could have been simply about the renovation, but like with many instances it also could have a double meaning.

"I wouldn't say that."

He held his arm out and I linked mine through. I didn't mind his dewy skin with a thin layer of sweat. I pulled my shirt away from my own sticky back. A nice cool shower would be my first order of business when I got home.

"You should talk to MJ."

"About what?"

"The wedding idea. He and his fiancée Olivia are in the early planning stages. I'm not sure they've even set a date yet."

I stopped walking. "Wait, your son is getting married?"

He shoved his hands into his back pockets and rocked back on his heels. "Yeah. Why do you sound so shocked?"

"I don't know, maybe because he seems so young."

Marcel shrugged. "They've been dating since they were sophomores in college. She's a sweet young lady, great head on her shoulders. She's a RN but has gone back to school to become a nurse anesthetist. When you think about it, if you...if things had been different, we would have probably married around that age or younger."

A new avalanche of guilt hit me. He turned and started back on the path toward the house, leaving me to scramble to catch up. How in the hell could he just drop a statement like that and then walk off?

"If you rather me ask him, I can. Porsha, Olivia, and her mom have been doing little bits and pieces."

The mention of his ex-wife was also so casual, as if the two of us talking was a normal occurrence. I certainly would not be calling her up to chat about anything.

When I was within reach, I grabbed his arm to stop him. "Don't you think that might be a tad bit weird?"

"What?"

"Me having any part of your son's wedding, first off. But even more, me having to make arrangements through your wife."

"Ex-wife. And no. Not weird for me. Porsha and I have been divorced for longer than we were married. She's been happily remarried for the last seven years. I think everyone will be thrilled at the idea of a stunning location on their budget. You said you needed a wedding. I'm trying to give you one."

Logical, problem-solving Marcel. Always and forever finding ways to take care of me. He made it sound so simple, and it could be. Things would only be weird if I made them that way. Weddings were big business, and having MJ be the first one on the grounds with his connection to everything made sense. And would be special. The more the possibility mulled around in my head, the more I got on board.

MARCEL

"Hey, Marcel," Regina greeted me when she opened the door.

I bent to give her a hug. "Evening, Gina." I handed her the bottles of wine.

"Ooh, you come with gifts. I'mma need to invite you over more often."

I laughed. "I wasn't sure if you ladies would want red or white, so I got both."

"And we'll drink both. Come on, she was plating when you rang the bell."

I took a deep inhale. "It smells good."

"Mm-hm. My girl's been cooking up a storm. Smothered pork chops, fried okra, rice, and cornbread. And your favorite, peanut butter and coconut cookies. Hey, Cyn, Marcel's here and he brought wine," she yelled out.

My steps faltered. It wasn't just the cookies that were my favorite. Cynthia had recreated the first meal she'd ever cooked for me. She'd remembered. It was a small thing, but at the same time not. I followed Regina into her large and well-appointed kitchen. She'd wanted top of the line everything when we'd remodeled it for her. Of all the pieces of furniture

I'd created, the range hood I'd crafted for her remained one of my favorites.

My attention went to Cynthia, who was setting the plates onto the table. Her silver hair was hidden beneath a multicolored silk scarf, and the simple pink paisley dress she wore looked like an oversized T-shirt. The cotton fabric clung to her curves when she moved. Curves I hadn't spent enough time getting reacquainted with.

Regina bumped me with her hip, the corner of her mouth quirked up on one side. "If you don't snatch her up, I might propose my damn self. She is straight spoiling me. You know how long it's been since someone else has cooked for me?"

Over the table, I locked eyes with Cynthia. "You probably stand a better chance of getting a yes," I replied, dragging my attention over to Regina.

Cynthia cleared her throat and released a low sigh. "Buying groceries and cooking is the least I can do since you won't let me pay you for staying here."

"Damn right I won't. What I look like charging you when I was the one to offer up? Besides, if the roles were reversed, you'd be the same damn way." Regina continued to fuss on her way to retrieve glasses and the corkscrew. She handed it to me. "You do the honors."

I uncorked the red and filled their glasses before doing my own. The ladies sat beside each other, and I took my place across from them. "This brings back memories."

Cynthia nodded slightly. "I've missed cooking for yo— people. Especially good o' Southern comfort food."

I couldn't keep the smile from tugging at my lips at her near slip up as I cut into my pork chop. My eyes rolled back when the well-seasoned, tender bite hit my taste buds. "Damn, woman. Let me just say, I'll willingly offer up myself for sacrifice anytime you get the itching to feed somebody."

"Sacrifice, huh?"

I put another delectable morsel into my mouth and

shrugged. "I mean, if someone needs to take one for the team, I'm sayin' I'm willin' is all."

Cynthia picked up her wine and shook her head, but I didn't miss the smile she tried to hide behind her glass.

After dinner, I insisted on doing the cleanup, not that they fought me too hard on it, and they went over her finishes and material options. Listening to them chatter in the background brought back the teenage memories. Hours spent sitting around Regina's or Irene's house. Or out at Ms. Drea's place. The three of them could talk for hours about everything and nothing. Some relationships were meant to stand the test of time. I glanced over my shoulder at the two of them. Their friendship was one of those relationships.

And some were not.

"You know, all he needs is an apron and one of those little maid caps. And when it's not my kitchen, maybe less clothes."

"Regina!" Cynthia admonished her friend.

I kept my back to them and pretended to not hear the direction of that conversation.

"What? Don't pretend you weren't thinking it."

"You're a whole ass mess." Humor was crystal clear in Cynthia's tone.

Voicing my lack of objection to Regina's statement was something I knew didn't need to be shared. With a sigh, I finished my task, tossed the dish towel over my shoulder, and turned to face them. "Got it all worked out?"

Cynthia ripped a page out of her notebook. "Yes, I believe we did. Sorry again for not doing this earlier." She handed me her choices, brushing her fingers against mine in the exchange.

I didn't believe in talks of soulmates and how some people were simply meant for each other. But as I stared into her honey-colored eyes, feeling the gravitational pull to her orbit, even with how things ended between us, my lack of belief had been issued a challenge.

"No worries. I got a meal and excellent company. Not a bad tradeoff for the delay."

Her full lips stretched into a warm grin. "If only dinner and conversation could work as an apology for all things."

"Yeah, if only."

She took an exaggerated breath and closed her eyes for half a second. "Um...do you need help carrying things out to your truck?"

She turned before I could answer and paused, tilting her head. Somehow, quickly and quietly, Regina had exited the kitchen and neither of us noticed. I folded the paper and slid it into my back pocket before joining Cynthia at the island. She stacked the cabinet, flooring, and countertop samples, ignoring me as I approached. I stood behind her, reaching out to place my hand over hers.

She stilled her actions. "Now is not the time," she whispered.

I trailed my fingers up her arm and embraced her, pulling her back against my body. "So when is? How long will we dance around the conversation we both know needs to be had?"

I spread my hand out atop her stomach and she covered it with her own. Closing my eyes, I matched my breathing to hers. Slow inhale. Slow exhale. The nagging questions bounced around in my head like an overactive toddler. Why? Why wouldn't she talk to me? Why did she need to leave like she did? The real reason, not the bullshit one she'd put in that fucking letter meant to cause maximum damage to my tender heart. Why wouldn't she let me be there for her?

She linked her fingers with mine and pulled my other arm around her so she was fully encased. "Can't we just... It's the past, Marcel. Choices made can't be undone. Can we just..."

I spun her to face me. "Can we what, Cyn? Move forward with whatever is happening here like nothing went down between us?"

She gazed up at me. Those beautiful eyes I could spend hours getting lost in were glazed in sadness. "Yes."

The single word came out just above a whisper and sent an arrow of rejection through my chest. I cupped her face, using my thumbs to stroke her cheeks. She curled her fingers around my wrists, and I leaned down and kissed her. Her soft lips familiar, yet not, beneath mine. Cynthia tilted her chin upward, and I resisted the urge to deepen the connection. Instead, I rested my head against her forehead.

"How can you expect me to do that?" I wanted this. I wanted us to have a potential second chance, but that couldn't happen with things unsettled. I pulled back and gathered my samples. "Will I see you tomorrow?"

She ran her fingers across her lips then pressed them together and crossed her arms. "Um, probably not. I have some things to work on. And I should stay out of the way."

The seconds ticked by with neither of us speaking.

Finally, I nodded. "Okay then. I should go. I'll get the stuff ordered. We shouldn't get behind on our schedule."

She followed me toward the front door. "Um, okay. I'm glad I didn't put you off...too much at least."

She'd thrown me off a hell of a lot, and I suspected that the added part had nothing to do with the work at the house. Cynthia opened her mouth as if to speak but said nothing. Instead, she reached around and opened the door for me.

"Goodnight, Marcel."

"Night."

As I walked to my truck, I got the sinking feeling that the soft click behind me signaled the closing of things between us before they'd gotten started.

❧ 20 ❧

CYNTHIA

I ADJUSTED THE ZOOM ON MY CAMERA TO BRING THE DUCKS swimming in the pond into focus. The park in the center of town was the gathering place of many community celebrations and having shots of it for my website made sense. I wanted the draw of the bed and breakfast to be more than just the house. Guests needed to be tempted to get out and explore the area.

My want to highlight different shops on my website was met with no resistance. Community. What was good for one, would be good for all. Or so the unofficial town motto went. I'd been sad to learn that Ms. Aubrey who'd owned Maids-a-Milkin' ice creamery had passed, but the new owners were a nice young couple.

I scrolled through my shots until I got to their smiling faces standing next to the "come on in" sign. They'd even suggested a few action shots of them making homemade milkshakes, and a picture-perfect banana split. They were the type of images that'd be great additions to my website to help sell not only the B&B, but Madison as a whole.

The cherry blossom trees were in full bloom, creating amazing background imagery. I let my camera dangle around my neck and rested against the trunk of one to take it all in. I'd forgotten how beautiful Madison was. How peaceful. People milled around, no one in a particular rush to get to where they were going. A couple having a picnic near the pond brought back memories. How many times had Marcel and I done that exact thing? *Marcel.* The desolate look in his eyes. The same look he'd had the night he'd first seen the tattoo.

My fear of seeing his disappointment in me was adding to the hurt I'd already caused him. I was once again being selfish and a coward. Hell, I'd even admitted to myself that it was something that needed to be done, yet avoidance of the topic seemed to be my go-to.

I was not that person. At least when I wasn't here. In Portland, I was direct. Said what needed to be said. Here, this place, this fucking town, it put me back into the box I'd so wanted out of.

But also here, here were people I cared about. People whose opinions of me mattered more than I wanted them to. One person's opinion. I closed my fingers around the cross at my neck. The ghosts of choices past would have to be faced.

I turned away from the couple and continued down the cobblestone path. Being back home had a calming effect, even if I was reluctant to admit it. The small town had a way of consistently emitting this "it's going to be okay" vibe. Maybe it was the air, or the unrushed, friendly attitude most the residents displayed, but something about this place made things seem possible. It lulled you into contentment. Which was the exact reason I'd needed away.

I snapped a few more shots of the park before making my way across the square to Just A Bit of Sugar. Lunch was the slower for them and the perfect time to get pictures of the building and my friend to include on the website. If she was providing key parts of the breakfast, I wanted folks to know. After getting what I needed outside, the bell above the door dinged when I entered.

Soft jazz poured through the speakers. The scent of sugar

and freshly brewed coffee swirled around, acting as a beacon to draw you closer to the display of stunningly beautiful confections. Nick, one of her employees I was getting to know, waved from his task of wiping down tables. Tricia smiled at me from behind the register. "Hey, Ms. Cynthia. What can I get you today?"

"Um, an apple fritter, bottle of water, and your boss."

I took a few shots of the pastries in the case before I settled at a table with my items and stared out the large window, watching the easy day go by.

"Cyn-Cyn."

I stood at the boisterous sound of Mama Charles. She pulled me into a tight embrace, then held me by the shoulders instead of releasing me completely. Wrinkles creased her forehead and a frowned tugged at her lips.

"How's Bishop Harris?"

I don't know why a question about my grandfather took me by surprise, but it did, especially coupled with her expression. My mother's father and my last remaining grandparent. And the man whose iron fist and strong convictions were the reason I was here and my parents had a loveless and tumultuous marriage.

For most people, fooling around at fifteen and sixteen was never supposed to lead to some sort of long-lasting commitment. Or, hell, any commitment at all. Unless that fifteen-year-old was the daughter of the town's reverend and she ended up pregnant. Sperm meeting egg had derailed two lives and made a third.

"Uh, as far as I know fine. I haven't gotten over to see any of them yet."

Her frown deepened. "I know you and your momma have issues, sweetie. But Madison ain't that big. You can't avoid them forever. At the service, he was on the sick and shut-in list, back in the hospital." She squeezed my shoulders before letting me go. However, the stern, yet motherly look held tight.

A tiny thread of guilt attempted to sew its way into my mind, but I couldn't let it. It's not like I had cut off all contact with them, I simply kept it to the bare minimum.

"I'll try and stop by." The words rang hollow in my ears since I knew damn well I had no intention of stepping foot in the hospital if I could avoid it. But I could at least call, or maybe ask Jennifer for an update.

No, shit, couldn't do that. Putting her in the middle of my family issues would be inappropriate. And I didn't need anyone else judging me over avoiding them. I'd figure out something later. My attention needed to be on my task at hand. "Are you going to be in my pictures?"

She fluffed at her gray-streaked curls. I was sure she still slept in rollers every night to achieve her signature hairstyle. "I don't know, don't want to outshine my girl."

"Isn't that what you live for?" Regina asked from behind. "That's why you insist on being here every day to harass me."

"Child, please, you know it's a privilege to see me every day and partake in all my knowledge."

Regina scoffed, but smiled wide. "Yeah, knowledge."

Their back and forth warmed my heart and made me the teeniest bit envious of their close relationship. Mama Charles had that same sort of attitude with her other children, but with Regina being the oldest their bond was different. Considering she was the only one interested in the family business helped that along. At least I suspected.

"Where do you want us?" Regina asked.

Her mom feigned complaints but happily smiled and posed for me. We said our goodbyes with me promising to join them for dinner. Papa Charles apparently had a good day out on the lake, which meant a fish fry was in order.

On my leisurely stroll down Main toward the square where I'd left my truck, my phone rang. A tiny spark of thrill hit thinking, hoping it'd be Marcel, but it fizzled out when the caller ID showed an unknown number.

"Hello?"

"Hi. Is this Cynthia?" the smooth, friendly female voice asked.

"It is. Who's speaking please."

"Yes. Hello. I'm Porsha Johnson. MJ's mother."

My steps faltered. Why in the hell would Marcel's wife—ex-wife, she was his ex—be calling me? And how? The shock gave way to anger if he'd given out my number and didn't have the decency to at least give me a fucking heads-up. And why would he do it?

"Hello? Are you there?"

"Yes, sorry. How can I help you?" I tried to keep my voice even as thoughts of the many choice words I'd have for Mr. Lewis after this call cycled through my head. I had nothing against the woman, but I also didn't see any reason for her to be dialing my phone.

"Yes, well I was talking to MJ last night, and he mentioned possibly having a location for his wedding. Imagine my surprise when he said it was the place he and his dad are currently renovating."

I massaged my temples as the conversation came back to me. Though I'd expected MJ, or hell, maybe even his fiancée to be the person to call, not her.

"Oh, yes. Cel mentioned they hadn't picked a venue. I want weddings to be one of the services, and he offered up your son's because I needed pictures for my website."

"I heard, which is why I'm calling. Are you free Saturday?"

I wandered over to one of the benches and took a seat. "As of right now, yes."

"Excellent. Two o'clock sound good? I would like to walk the property, check things out. I'm acting as sort of their unofficial wedding planner."

"Uh...sure."

"Great. See you then. I can't wait to meet you."

"Same."

Once the call ended, I remained on the bench, attempting to

wrap my head around what had just happened. Not only had I had a conversation with the ex-Mrs. Lewis, I had agreed to a face-to-face meeting with her in a few days' time. She sounded pleasant enough, but Marcel still needed to answer for not so much as sending me a text that she might call. And would he be at that meeting?

Standing, I refused to analyze the conflicted feelings taking hold at the thought of witnessing Marcel in family man mode.

MARCEL

THE SOFT WHISPER OF SANDPAPER AGAINST MAPLE ALWAYS PUT me at ease. Softening the rounded edges, making sure the cuts made were smooth to the touch, all the little stops on the journey. I never grew tired of watching a new project take shape, moving from a basic piece of wood into something meaningful. Something useful.

I loved my job. I loved being part of a major change in people's lives, helping them get the most out of their home or business. Being around to see the joy on their faces, and receiving their accolades for a job well done, all of it was a great reward. But creating special pieces, something handcrafted and personalized with no one but the recipient in mind, doing those put me in a zen-like state.

And I needed all the zen I could get today.

I blew, sending small particles of dust swirling into the air. When Porsha had called to not only tell me she and Alicia were coming, but why, my stress level had spiked. So much so that I gave the crew the day off because I didn't need them around to speculate or gossip about anything. Plus, it meant I could spend my morning alone, just me and the wood. The calming solitude to mentally prepare for the face-to-face with my ex. Both my exes, if I were being honest.

It wasn't like I expected either of them to be catty, but that didn't mean I wanted them talking without a buffer, at least to start with. Especially considering Cynthia had already hinted at reservations, but MJ blew that whole idea out of the water with him freely giving his mother Cyn's number. I'd chuckled, watching the realization dawn on him after both Olivia and I explained why it might not have been the best idea.

The alarm on my phone sounded. I took off my safety goggles and pulled the device from my pocket. One hour 'til the meet. I had time to do a quick cleanup of the shop and then one for myself.

⌘

WHEN I ARRIVED at the house, Cynthia's truck was already parked. Figured she'd be early. Punctuality, one of the things we had in common. Movement in the upper window caught my eye. Leaning forward, I squinted and peered over my steering wheel to find Cynthia staring in my direction. She waved, and that small acknowledgment was encouraging since her attitude had been cool at best when we'd talked. I suspected MJ apologizing for his oops had something to do with that.

She was coming down the stairs as I entered the house, and man was she a sight for sore eyes. I'd not seen her since dinner at Regina's, and being in her presence now... Damn, I'd missed her. The deep-purple halter-top sundress she wore looked amazing against her skin. It was cinched at her waist, and the flowy material kissed her curves and made it look as if she were gliding since it fell all the way to the floor. She completed the outfit with a wide brim straw sunhat with a band of matching purple fabric.

"You look nice."

She glanced down briefly. "Just nice? With the way you were

staring at me, I figured I'd get something a little more eloquent." Her full lips stretched into a smile to match the amused glint in her eyes.

I hooked my sunglasses on the neck of my shirt and stepped closer. I slipped one arm around her waist, tugging her body flush to mine. "You are a vision to behold. Watching you move in this stunningly sexy ensemble is hypnotic, and I happily and willingly fall under your spell. I find myself jealous of the fabric because it gets to be so close to your beautiful body. Especially since I've gotten reacquainted with the delights it covers and knowing how absolutely magical they are."

Her lips parted and her eyes dilated.

I leaned and placed a chaste kiss below her ear and whispered, "Eloquent enough?" As much as I wanted to kiss her while running my hands under that damn dress to make her come all over my fingers, I stepped away.

Cynthia stumbled back and gripped the bannister. Any reply she might have made was denied by the sound of gravel crunching beneath tires. I held my hand out for her. She glanced at her bag that hung on the newel post and apparently made the split-second decision to leave it when she took me up on my offer.

I curled my fingers around hers and squeezed. "This will be fine."

My family piled out of MJ's car, and Cynthia tensed beside me.

"Afternoon, Ms. Cynthia," MJ greeted. "This is my fiancée, Olivia."

Cynthia released my hand to shake my future daughter-in-law's.

"I've been here for years and never knew about this house," Olivia commented, glancing up at the large Victorian.

"Daddy!" Alicia squealed, blazing between her brother and Olivia to launch herself at me. I knew her extra excitement was partly due to the hopes I'd buy her a new car instead of getting her other one fixed, and partly her genuine enthusiasm at seeing me. She was unabashedly a daddy's girl.

"Hey, baby girl. How you feeling?"

"Fine other than not having any transportation." She pouted and folded her arms across her chest.

I pinched her chin. "Chin up, baby girl. You'll be back to being a menace to drivers soon enough."

Her brother laughed. She huffed but gave me a smile. I placed my hand on her lower back and gently pushed her closer to Cynthia.

"Cyn, this is my baby girl, and the reason all my hair fell out." Alicia playfully swatted my stomach when I said that. "Alicia, this is my old...friend, Cynthia Marshall."

My daughter lowered her shades and peered at me over them, then turned her radiant smile toward Cynthia.

"Nice to meet you."

My attention went to Porsha. She'd hung back, standing just behind our son. That fact alone concerned me. Porsha being somewhat reserved and laid back? The behavior didn't compute, and I was waiting on the universe to implode from her chillness. I couldn't see her eyes because of the large designer sunglasses, but when she turned in my direction, she gave a slight nod and a smile. I could only imagine what she'd have to say over dinner tonight. She approached and hesitated half a second before engulfing me in a hug as usual. Then she turned, moved her shades so they sat on the brim of the baseball cap she wore, and faced off with my other ex. I exchanged tentative glances with my children.

"Cynthia, so nice to meet you."

"Likewise."

Cynthia extended her hand, which Porsha ignored and instead went in for a hug. And there was the Porsha I knew. The outgoing, and overly friendly woman I'd once been married to. There wasn't a stranger Porsha didn't like until you gave her a reason to. Cynthia's eyes went wide as she awkwardly returned the embrace.

An odd Twilight Zone moment was happening. Standing on the property where I'd spent a good portion of my youth, my two pasts colliding. I'd never been a man to play the field. My parents had provided me with a happy and loving home, and that had been something I'd wanted to recreate in my own life. I'd loved Cynthia, and she'd broken my heart. I'd loved Porsha, and while I'd seen the end of our marriage coming a mile away, the loss of it had also broken a piece of me.

Two women who'd been important in shaping who I was and who remained integral parts of my life. Having them both here, in this moment, I hadn't realized before that having them not only meet, but also hopefully get along was a necessity, even if albeit a slightly selfish one.

CYNTHIA

I HADN'T BEEN SURE WHAT TO EXPECT FROM PORSHA. SHE WAS stunningly beautiful, reminding me of Iman. While I'd thought MJ to be a clone of his father, upon meeting his mother I certainly saw her genes in his features. And their daughter... She was model material having gained Marcel's smooth, dark complexion and height mixed with her mother's brown hair and high cheekbones. Marcel had a gorgeous family, and the young lady marrying into it would fit right in.

The anxiety and uncertainty I'd had since setting up this meeting lessened. I couldn't keep letting myself get caught up in the what-ifs of what we could have been. The negative thoughts and worries since coming back and the tension-filled moments we'd had fueled those. Yes, I may have hurt him by leaving, but staying would have denied him the love and family he'd had in my absence.

I turned to face MJ and Olivia. "Do you want to see the location I was thinking would work first? Or tell me what you had in mind?"

"I think the spot," Olivia answered.

Marcel placed his hand on my lower back and directed me forward with the rest of them following. I tried not to focus on what his children, mostly his daughter, thought of his slight display of affection. Both Irene and Regina were very much daddy's girls, and the small interaction I witnessed between Marcel and Alicia led me to believe she was as well.

As we approached the open space, the freshly cut grass wasn't missed on me. I shot a quick glance over to Marcel, who simply smiled. On top of the work they'd done on the house, he'd apparently found time to tame the somewhat unruly yard. It was those little things, the knowing what's needed and doing it without fanfare or expecting anything in return. Some things had changed with him, but so much had remained the same.

Porsha stepped forward and started taking pictures on her phone. "What do you think, Liv, MJ? The location is beautiful. Peaceful. You have a great piece of property here."

"Thank you. I spent a lot of time here in my younger days."

She smiled and nodded. I noticed how her gaze went to Marcel's arm, which was still prominently around my waist before she walked toward where two of the large mossy oaks stood.

"And right here I can see some sort of arch or something where you'd exchange the vows."

The happy couple agreed with her assessment, talking placement, and they all seemed to be into it.

"Daddy, you should build it," Alicia chimed in. "I mean how cool would it be for them to get married under something you made."

The rest of his family all lit up at the idea and fell into agreement.

Marcel moved so that he could center himself between the two trees. He held his hands up, creating a frame, and closed one eye. "Yeah, I could probably do that."

Excitement all around, and it warmed my heart to see MJ embrace his father in thanks, followed by Marcel's soon to be daughter-in-law. Tears pricked the back of my eyes thinking about how excited Auntie would have been to finally host a wedding here. Sure, it wouldn't be the one she'd hoped for, but it was close, considering it would be Marcel's son.

Porsha clapped her hands. "Well, ladies and gents, sounds like we finally have a location. Now these two need to settle on a date." She gave them a pointed look then turned her attention to me. "We didn't talk numbers on the phone, but did you have a fee in mind?"

All eyes went to me.

"I wasn't planning on charging for use of the land since having it here helps me out if MJ and Olivia don't mind some of their wedding being used on my website. So, really, it'd be simply paying whatever event company for tents, chairs, that sort of thing."

I found myself engulfed in a hug from MJ. "Ms. Cynthia, you sure?"

I met Marcel's gaze over MJ's shoulder, and the grin on his face couldn't have been wider.

"Yeah, I'm happy to help make your upcoming day one to remember."

The mood was jubilant as we started walking back. MJ poked fun at his father being an old man after Alicia jumped on Marcel's back for a piggyback ride. Watching him interact with his children left me with mixed emotions. I'd always known he'd make an excellent father, and part of me wished I could have somehow witnessed his greatness when they were younger. He'd probably not missed a single game or event they were in. That had been the life he'd wanted with me. And the life I'd tried to tell myself I was okay with, until I'd been faced with that real possibility.

"Do you have kids?"

I'd been so caught up in my thoughts, I'd not noticed Porsha had fallen into step with me.

I shook my head, casting a fleeting look in Marcel's direction before turning to her. "Uh, no. Children weren't part of my life plan."

"Huh. I can understand that. I hadn't put much thought into it before I married Marcel. But..." She extended her arm out in the direction where the others waited for us, still joking around. "He was certainly daddy material, though two was my limit. But I have three now since my current husband has a son from his previous marriage. Blending a family can have some hiccups, but you can get through it long as all parties are on the same page."

Having this strange heart-to-heart conversation with Marcel's ex-wife was a little disconcerting. She'd been nice, but my general unease about this meeting had me on edge waiting to see if claws were going to come out for some reason. Especially since she'd stopped walking and we were just out of earshot of the group.

I didn't know this woman, and I was not one to be baring my soul on why children weren't something I wanted. The defensiveness sat at the tip of my tongue, but I took in a slow breath to calm myself.

"Look, I'm sure you know that I know you and Marcel used to date. And if this rekindling goes anywhere, congrats it's a boy *and* a girl. I get the feeling from today that you'd be a good addition to their lives. Don't prove me wrong."

Ah, it might have been wrapped up in a friendly-ish message, but I was being put on notice where her children were concerned. I couldn't even get mad over that. Regina was the same way with Darnell. Though some of that was due to the fact she could have lost both her son and her husband the night of the crash.

Marcel and Porsha had a good thing going. And it wasn't something you saw often with divorced couples. He was a package deal, regardless of how old MJ and Alicia were. He was a father of two, and to be in his life meant being in theirs.

"You two over here talking about me?" Marcel asked on his approach.

I turned to face him. "Why would you think we'd be talking about you?" I slipped some humor into my tone.

"Um, because I'm an interesting topic."

Porsha laughed. "Says you."

"You know what, the only person I'm taking out to dinner is Olivia since she's the nice one. The rest of you can fend for yourself."

Porsha waved him off while shaking her head. "Whatever. Where are they anyway?"

"MJ is giving them a tour of the house."

They were coming out as we approached the cars.

"You can guess what Pizza Monster here wants for dinner," MJ said, pointing his thumb toward his sister.

"Sounds good. Cynthia, will you be joining us?" Porsha asked.

I glanced toward Marcel then back to his ex-wife. I know he'd said interacting with his ex wasn't weird. They had a good post-marriage relationship and it made me wonder about her new husband. There was a clear dynamic between Marcel, Porsha, and their children. How had he fit into that? Whatever Marcel and I were possibly rebuilding was still on a shaky foundation, would dinner with them have me under a microscope?

"I don't want to impose."

She waved off my answer. "It's not an imposition. We'd love you to join us. Can do more wedding talk."

I stole another glance at Marcel who'd remained quiet. "Thank you. I'll try to make it."

They said their goodbyes, the group making sure I knew the invite to dinner was open. As soon as their car was down the drive Marcel pulled me into his arms.

"Was that as worrisome as you'd imagined?"

I shook my head and rested my palms against his chest. "No, you have a beautiful family. You're very lucky. Even your ex is nice."

He opened and closed his fingers along my lower back, creating a soft tickling sensation.

"What was that about anyway?"

"What was what about?"

His dark shades hid his eyes, but the slight tilting of his head was signal enough that he didn't buy my "playing dumb" act.

"Nothing. She was just thanking me again for the use of the property."

He looked down, peering at me over the glasses. "Okay. And about that, you have to let me pay you."

"You can't expect me to take your money."

He stepped back and crossed his arms. "I'm taking yours." He pointed his chin in the direction of the house.

I planted my hands on my hips. "That's different. If I'd called you over to unclog the sink, that would be one thing. You are doing a full-blown renovation, which involves your crew, materials, time. I would never expect that for nothing. But if it makes you feel better, I won't pay you for cutting the grass."

He took his shades off and hooked them on the collar of his shirt. He rolled his tongue between his lips before putting his dazzlingly white teeth on display. Marcel stepped closer, placing his hands on my waist. "How do you know that was me?"

"Are you denying it?"

"Depends."

"On?"

"What kind of thank-you I get."

His lips descended on mine, and he swept his tongue through my mouth before I could even formulate a response. My brain tried to understand how he could be on me like a starving man after his family had just left, but it was drowned out by the part of me that had wanted this earlier. Between the huskiness of his voice, the lust in his words when he'd complimented me, and the general sexiness of Marcel in a fitted V-neck T-shirt and a pair of shorts that showed off his toned legs and tight ass, it all had me wishing for a repeat of our night together.

His large hands palmed my behind, gathering the fabric of my dress until he got to the flesh beneath it. I melded my body to his and let the need take control.

A deep groan rumbled in the back of his throat before he

broke from the kiss and let my dress fall. Marcel rested his forehead on mine. "I better stop now before I have you bent over in my truck."

I wiggled free and left him calling out behind me as I scurried into the house where my bag remained. I returned, proudly holding up a small black cosmetic pouch. "I'm not entirely opposed to that idea. And thanks to Regina, I now am the proud new owner of a sex-on-the-go survival kit."

I'd laughed off the idea when she'd given it to me, but now I was immensely thankful for her intuitive thinking. Marcel's lustful grin made me even more thankful that I'd actually put it in my purse instead of leaving it at home.

MARCEL

THE SEXY SWAY OF HER HIPS AS SHE SAUNTERED TOWARD ME was its own form of foreplay. That pouch in her hand was a life-saver, though we'd have to have another talk at a later date since pregnancy was not a concern thanks to my vasectomy, and before she showed back up, it'd been over a year since I was last with someone.

When she was in reach, I wrapped my arm around her waist and took full advantage of her soft lips again. My dick twitched when I remembered how good that same mouth had felt when she'd sucked me off. Fumbling behind me, I managed to get the door of my truck open. She handed me the black pouch, and with a coy smile firmly in place, kept her eyes on me as she gathered the fabric of her dress and removed her panties.

"You said something about having me bent over. What's the hold up?"

I didn't think I could get any harder, but damn was I wrong. The foxy vixen maneuvered herself between me and the truck, lifted her dress to reveal her bare ass, then leaned forward to rest her elbows on the driver's seat.

My shorts were unbuttoned and both they and my boxer briefs were at my ankles in record time. The handy kit contained condoms, lube, and wipes. I kissed her exposed back as I rolled the condom on, slathering some additional lubricant since there hadn't been proper foreplay. And I slid home.

She immediately constricted her walls around me, like an erotic hug. The sensation threatening to have things over before they really got started.

"Fuck, baby," I groaned, slamming into her again.

I gripped Cynthia's waist. The hot Georgia sun beat down on us. Sweat trickled down my back. The sound of our flesh slapping together mingled with our grunts and groans disrupted the peaceful setting. The sight of her upturned ass plus her whimpering pleas for more pushed me closer and closer to release.

I slipped a hand between her legs and made circles around her clit.

"God, yes. Like that. Faster. Faster," she begged.

I fed her demands, rubbing her stiff nub harder as I continued to pound into her slick body. Cynthia pressed her arms against the console and let out a drawn-out, "Fuck." Her leg shook, and the tiny convulsions of her orgasm brought my own forward. I squeezed her ass as my release flooded the latex barrier.

I slumped over her and pressed my lips to her sweat-covered shoulder. With another squeeze to her delectable ass, I pulled out. It'd been a minute since I'd had spontaneous quick and dirty sex. Letting go and giving into the lustful, primal need with nothing more on my mind than the physical need and connection. Doing so with Cynthia took me back to a simpler time.

"Next time we do something like this, it needs to be winter so I don't damn near end up with heat stroke," she stated with a laugh.

I chuckled and nodded in agreement while not trying to zone in too much on the "next time" part of her statement. She pulled two wipes from the pouch and handed me one. Her hair was messed up from the hat and then it being knocked off. Perspiration dotted her forehead, but she looked stunning all the same.

After discarding the condom and wipes, I returned from the house with her purse and two bottles of water the crew kept in a cooler. Cynthia sat in the very seat she'd just been bent over, hat back in place, eyes closed, and contentment on her face. My ego inflated at having had a hand in that.

"Figured you could use this," I said, handing her the bottle. "And brought this out since I locked up for you." I set her bag on the floorboard.

"Comes so natural."

"What?"

"You, taking care of people. Me." She fiddled with the cap of her bottle when she said the last part.

"It's what I'm good at." Stepping forward, I slid the silky fabric of her dress up to her thighs and settled between her legs. "Will you come to dinner?"

She took a long drink of water and dabbed her mouth with the back of her hand. "Don't you want some alone time with your family?"

I placed my bottle on the floor then slid my hands around her waist. "Is there a reason you're trying to get out of joining us?"

"Look, I know how these things go. I'm sure they want time to talk about me. To get a feel of how serious or not serious Dad is about this new woman. The invite was one of those polite gestures."

"You're wrong. The invite was and is genuine. Sure, Alicia might be curious, but I can guarantee she's already hit her brother up for information since he's been around you and us. But if you're worried about issues, don't be. Both of them are basically grown. Neither have any ideas of their mother and I ever remarrying. No worries about them trying to do some TV drama sabotage or anything."

"You say that, but I know how girls can be about their daddies. Maybe not from personal experience, but still, I've seen it."

My old resentment flared at the small dig she'd made about her relationship with her father. It was hard to say which was worse, the constant put downs from her mother, or her father's indifference. For so long she tried to hide how much her parents affected her, pretending it didn't matter, when in fact it had mattered quite a lot.

As a teen I couldn't fathom it in comparison to how my own parents treated me and my siblings. We were their world. As a father myself, I'd found it even harder to imagine how they could inflict the sort of pain they had on Cynthia.

My family was my everything. I trailed my fingers down her arms until I held both her hands in mine. Staring into her warm brown eyes, it dawned on me that while I didn't see an issue, it could be overwhelming for her. Having dinner with my kids, Porsha, and sometimes her husband was a normal occurrence whenever we were in the same city. Being a cohesive and amicable family unit was something we'd collectively strived for. On the outside, Vince didn't seem to show any reservations, but who knew what conversations he and Porsha had in the beginning.

"Cyn, I would like for you to come, but I understand if you'd rather not. No pressure." I leaned to give her a chaste kiss. "Where are your keys?"

She frowned. "Why are you stealing my truck?"

"If I was, would I ask for the keys? Now, hand them over."

She did as asked, and I jogged over to crank it up and get the AC going for her. When I returned, I reached around her and did the same to mine.

"What time are y'all meeting for dinner?"

"Not sure. They will all probably be at the house when I get there."

She turned her face toward the air vent, closed her eyes, and let the coolness hit her skin for a few minutes before moving to climb down from the seat. "I need to shower and see what Regina is up to. I'll text you, though."

Wasn't a yes, but it also wasn't a no, so I'd take it. She stretched up, and I met her for the kiss she was after. Greedily, I watched the sway of her hips and the movement of her ass on her journey to her vehicle. When she climbed in, the relief of the cooled space showed on her face, which brought a smile to mine.

She was right; taking care of her did come natural. Once again, the memories ping-ponged in my head. The what-ifs clawed their way back to the surface. And I couldn't help but wonder how much longer we'd dance around the elephant between us.

She waved before putting it in reverse and driving off, and I shook free the thoughts. A shower was certainly in order, and it would help me get my head right before dinner. As I climbed into my seat, fabric on the passenger side caught my eye. Reaching over, I retrieved the light pink cotton, bringing it to my nose for a deep inhale. I glanced up in the rearview mirror where only a small cloud of dust remained of Cyn's departure.

I didn't know if they were left on accident or not, but I stuffed my find into my pocket all the same. Finders keepers.

❧ 24 ❧

CYNTHIA

I KEPT A SMILE ON MY FACE THE ENTIRE DRIVE HOME thinking about Marcel's possible reaction when he found my panties. Was I too old to be doing silly things like leaving my underwear behind after having sex in his car? Probably so. But was it fun to do it all the same? Hell yes. When I wasn't over-thinking every little damn thing, being around him was easy. Relaxed. And it brought out the fun, playful side of me.

The sight of Regina's car in the garage took me by surprise. She normally closed down the bakery regardless of how many times me and Irene told her she was going to burn herself out with constant twelve-plus-hour days. Over the years, she and her family had built up a solid team, but Regina always felt like she had something more to prove. Especially with her siblings off doing other things and making lives for themselves away from Madison.

"Hey girl, what..." My words died off at the sight of my friend sitting at the island with a bottle of bourbon. I dropped my bag on the counter and rushed to her side. "What happened?"

My heart raced, fearing the worst. Had something happened to her parents or Darnell?

"He's been stealing from me."

"Who?"

She slid a thick folder over to me as I took a seat on the stool beside her. I didn't understand a lot of what I was looking at, but it appeared to be receipts of orders with lines highlighted and spreadsheets of profits and losses with notes in the margins and discrepancies circled.

"Fucking Trent, that's who. That bastard has been with us for years. Years! And he does this shit."

He was her right-hand man for the most part. Stepping in to take on more of the managerial roles around the bakery, especially after her mom retired. My blood started to boil at the idea of him taking advantage of her and her family. And I was ready to go and beat his ass for the distress he was causing her.

"I don't get it, Gina. What is all of this?"

She drained the rest of the amber liquid from her glass and poured a refill. "I've been having to meet with my accountant because I'm getting audited. No big deal...until she started checking through things just to make sure every I was dotted and T was crossed." Again, she downed the contents of her glass in one gulp. "Who'd have fucking thought the motherfucking IRS would be the reason I learned I was being fucking swindled?" She let out a sardonic laugh.

I flipped through the file again, trying to make sense of the numbers. Based on the dates on the receipts, it'd been going on for about two years. How her accountant hadn't caught it sooner was a question for another day. For the moment, my friend needed my shoulder to cry on, and my mutual anger and disgust that a person could do something like this to her.

"If he needed money, all he had to do was ask. We woulda worked something out. All he had to do was say. But to fucking steal from me. From my momma. From a business we've worked our asses off to make successful. And the worst part is, I trusted him. The one fucking time I try to take a step back, to be okay having help or whatever, and this shit happens."

Regina poured herself another drink. I got up to fill a glass with some water. She'd thank me for it later. I grabbed the bourbon and gulped it down, wincing as the bitter liquid burned my throat. She frowned at me for stealing her drink but began sipping on the water anyway.

"I'm allowed to drown my sorrows, you know."

I wrapped my arms around her shoulders and pulled her to me. "Yes, you are, and you can, soon as we get back."

"Back? Where we going?"

"It's theft. On a somewhat medium to large-ish scale if I'm reading those papers right. We need to see the sheriff so you can file a report."

Small town life had its perks, one of which included knowing people in "high" places. But in the case of Sheriff Frederick Parker, Regina had an extra leg up with the man being her father-in-law. If anyone would be as eager to see Trent brought to justice as I was, it'd be Sheriff Parker.

She pushed away and started shaking her head. "I can't." She held up her hand to stop my impending protest. "At least not yet. My accountant is going through all the records from since Trent was hired just to see if maybe he'd tried something before and it slipped through the cracks. Then I'll go to Pops."

Resting against the granite, I crossed my arms and ventured toward my earlier unspoken question. "How was it missed in the first place?"

She shook her head. "I don't know. Leslie is my new one. Our old accountant had been doing our books for years but should have retired back when Gram did. Now his ass is RVing across the country or something. But he never said a thing, and I'm left with this mess. Which is why Leslie is going back farther to see what's what."

She pressed her palms to her eyes and took in a deep, shuddering breath. Once again, I embraced my friend. Regina was a woman who prided herself on being strong. On having it all together and not letting things get to her or in the way. She didn't like to show weakness, so it took a hell of a lot for the walls to crumble and the emotions to be openly displayed. But that bastard had done it and I could honestly say I hated him for it.

"It's gon' be okay, Regina. We will get through this."

My heart ached for her. I knew the pain she was experiencing. I'd had the same disbelief and sadness when I'd been laid off, but for my friend, it cut deeper. It was more personal. To think people were loyal and trustworthy only to have the rug pulled out from under her. Like she'd said, if Trent had been having money issues, they would have helped. Resorting to stealing was low and a deep betrayal. Fury, sorrow, incredulity all crashed through me as my friend softly cried in my arms.

Being back home had brought up a ton of mixed feelings, but in this moment, I was thankful I could be with my friend in her time of need. Regina was a strong, proud woman, so I knew how deep the wound would be. Her family was tight knit; they'd band together and survive, and I'd help in any way I could. Even if that meant simply holding her while she let the pain out.

૭૪૭

A JACKHAMMER WAS GOING full blast in my head as I cracked my eyes open with a groan before quickly squeezing them shut again. I grabbed the end of my pillow and folded it over my offending dome as I rolled to the side.

It'd been a long-ass time since I'd drank that much, and hard liquor at that. But Regina had wanted to drown her sorrows, and boy oh boy had we done that. My bladder screamed out for relief, and I desperately needed to rid myself of the fuzzy taste in my mouth. As I shuffled down the hall, there was no scent of coffee or freshly baking pastries. No signs of life at all. She was probably still sleeping it off.

She'd needed last night. To get completely shit-faced while

raging at the situation. And I'd stayed by her side talking shit about the evil bastard while reminding her she wasn't alone and didn't have to deal with it all on her own.

Bladder emptied and mouth minty fresh, I quietly made my way to the kitchen. The soft clink of the mugs hitting together might as well have been them all crashing to the floor with how the sound seemed magnified to my sensitive ears. I tried my best to ease the ceramic noise makers onto the granite countertop.

I eyed the coffee grinder with disdain and was happy that I'd had the foresight to buy some ground after one too many mornings silently cursing that machine. I was invading her space, so I tried not to complain, but yeah, me and the coffee grinder didn't get along. With the aromatic scent of deep roast filtering through the air, I settled onto her plush sofa and waited for my rich headache-ridder to finish brewing.

I rested my head back and let the soothing sounds of the maker seep into my weary soul.

"Bless you." Regina's voice made me jump.

I pushed off the couch. "Thought you'd sleep a little longer."

"I'm used to getting up." Her stomach grumbled causing us both to laugh. "Plus, as you can hear, I'm hella hungry."

The final sputters of the coffee maker were a welcomed signal to both of us. Regina filled the two mugs while I headed over to the fridge to retrieve some creamer along with bacon and eggs for breakfast.

"Mmm, heaven in a cup." She sighed after taking her first sip. "So, how was it? I was so caught up last night I didn't even ask."

I stirred in my cream and sugar and took my own glorious first taste. I closed my eyes and let the sweet, hot liquid permeate my senses. "How was what?"

"Meeting Porsha."

"Oh, shit."

I set my cup down and dashed over to where my purse, and subsequently, my phone remained from the previous night. The mention of Porsha's name reminded me that I was supposed to have dinner, or at the very least let Marcel know for sure one way or another.

"What's wrong?"

I dug around in my bag until I found the device. Sure enough, I had missed calls, text messages, and one voicemail. "Damn it. It's nothing really. I was invited to dinner with them last night and then with everything..." I dialed into my voicemail.

"Hey, Cyn. I'm going to hope everything is okay and you have a good excuse for standing me up and ignoring my attempts to get in touch with you. Because last time you went radio silent... Anyway, call me when you get this."

My heart sank. The message wasn't rude, per se, but there was an unmistakable edge laced in his monotone words. The dig about me going radio silent...he had to know I wouldn't just disappear like that again. I was in the middle of a renovation, for goodness sake.

"Call him, it'll be fine."

The construction crew in my head ramped up their pounding, causing pain to shoot down my neck and prickle behind my eyes. It was a simple explanation, and one he would easily accept. Regina had needed me, and in the crisis I'd simply forgotten to call him. I'd simply forgotten about him...*Shit.* The guilt returned. Every melancholy expression that had passed across Marcel's face since my return. Every snide comment which gave me a minor glimpse of the pain I'd caused him. Each one gnawed at me, prickled beneath my skin, and made my heart constrict.

"I'll do it after breakfast." Though my stomach lurched, rejecting the idea of food.

"Uh-huh. I can get the bacon started, you go return his call."

I wanted to argue and tell her it could wait. Instead, I headed over toward the living room. He deserved better than my continued cowardice.

"Hey, Cyn?"

"Yeah?"

"Thanks, though. Having you here last night helped."

I smiled at my friend. "No thanks needed. There was nowhere else I would have been." *But I should have let him know.*

❦ 25 ❦

MARCEL

I RINSED THE FINAL PAN AND LOADED IT INTO THE dishwasher.

"Did you leave me any?"

I turned to face my daughter as she stifled a yawn.

"Yeah, you have a plate in the microwave. What do you want to do today?"

She hit "Start" to heat up her food before moving over to pull the tea from the cabinet and flick on the kettle. She may not have lived with me full time, but I made sure she felt like this place was just as much home as her mother's.

The microwave beeped. She retrieved her food and headed over to the table. "Depends on what time Mom wants to head back," she answered around a forkful of eggs. "Will our time include your new lady friend?"

I chuckled at the use of her term as I poured the hot water into the awaiting mug then carried it and the honey over to the table. "I don't think so. Why?"

She shrugged and squeezed a copious amount of the sticky sweetener into her cup. "I just figured you two had to be serious or something."

I rested my forearms on the table and leaned forward. "Why would you think that?"

Her signature eye roll was accompanied with a loud and overly dramatic sigh. "Mom didn't stay here like she normally does. And..." She took another bite of eggs, which came across as a small delay tactic.

"And what?"

My phone chose that moment to ring. We both turned to look at the contraption where it sat plugged in on the counter.

"You should get that. It might be important."

"You're important."

She smiled and took a sip of her tea while shifting her eyes over toward the noise-making device.

"Fine." I shoved my chair back, ready to tell whoever was on the other end I'd call them back later. Cynthia's name flashing on the screen switched my annoyance at the interruption to temporary relief she'd at least not fled this time. Or if she had, at least I was getting the courtesy of a phone call.

I unplugged it and hit the little green phone icon. "Hello."

"Good morning."

"Same to you."

There was an awkward pause, and from the corner of my eye I saw Alicia pretending to not be interested in my conversation. They'd all asked about Cynthia last night, and it had irritated me that I couldn't even give a real answer on why she wasn't there.

"I'm sorry about last night. Something came up with Regina."

I took a steadying breath and walked down the hall. "You could have at least sent a text."

"I know. I'm sorry. It was a crisis, and I got so caught up with being there for her that I just forgot."

I understood the closeness of her friendship. They were like the Three Musketeers back in the day, and time hadn't changed that. Three simple words—"I just forgot"—but complicated enough to remind me some things, or better yet someone, could so easily slip out of her mind. Once more, I was transported back to eighteen-year-old me, battling the ache and unease.

"You there?"

I rubbed at the tension in the back of my neck. "Yeah. Is everything okay now?"

She paused. In the background I could hear pots and muffled singing.

"Not yet, but we're working on it."

There was strain in her voice. A weariness that, despite my own feelings, made me want to take her stress away. I'd spent a large part of my youth doing just that. Trying to lessen her burden and find ways to bring a smile to her beautiful face.

"Is there anything I can do?"

Another pause. "I don't know. A lot depends on Regina. I can't really say more since it's not my place."

I understood the message loud and clear. Their friend code of silence was strong. Unbreakable. Something I remembered from when she'd disappeared. Neither of them would put me out of my misery and had only offered up platitudes.

"Got it. Well, I should let you go. Alicia's here, and we were in the middle of something when you called."

"Okay. And, Marcel, I had every intention of going last night. I was looking forward to getting to know your family better."

Some of the boulders in my stomach dissipated from her admission. Though regardless of how I tried to ignore the nagging in the back of my mind her words repeated again. "I just forgot." About me. About us. About our plans.

"Maybe next time."

Hushed whispers and sounds of fumbling. "How about lunch? My treat."

An effort? As much as the possibility alleviated more of my discomfort, her actions from the previous night gave me a moment of pause. Reminding me there was much between us which remained unsettled. "I don't know. Let me see what everyone's plans are, and I'll get back to you."

"Okay. And again, I'm sorry about last night."

"I'll call you later."

After we disconnected, I took a few calming breaths before heading back to my daughter.

"Trouble in paradise already?" she asked on her journey to her favorite corner of my sectional. She'd claimed the spot as hers the day we'd picked it out.

"There is no paradise. Now, back to what we were talking about."

Alicia reached for the remote. "It's nothing." She grabbed the blanket from the back of the sofa and wrapped it around her bare legs.

I settled back against the plush cushions and watched her as she flipped through the channels. Hard to believe that in a few short weeks she'd be graduating high school. My last one. My baby girl, moving on to the next phase of her life. Reaching over, I gave her foot a squeeze. There was something in her tone and demeanor that offset her nonchalant attitude.

"Alicia."

She huffed in dramatic fashion. "Daddy, it's nothing. I mean, it's good you have someone to grow old, or rather, *older* with."

"Alicia Renee Lewis, quit blowing smoke."

She pulled up the blanket and tucked it around her chest while crossing her arms. The move was accompanied with a semi-pout.

"Fine. Since you're doing that whole stern voice, full-name parent thing." After another full, drawn out sigh she spoke again. "She's the first."

"First what?"

"Person you've dated or whatever that you've introduced us to. Plus, like I said, Mom has always stayed here. I mean, sure, before MJ didn't have a place yet, but even still... So we just assumed you and Ms. Cynthia must be serious."

I thought back over the last ten years. I'd done the whole online dating thing mostly thanks to Jennifer insisting I needed to "get back out there" and had reluctantly gone on a few dates when a new nurse or whoever joined the hospital. My sister was forever trying to set me up, but luckily that died off a few years after the divorce.

"I'm sure there've been others."

She shook her head. "Nope." She added an extra pop to the P. "MJ and I talked. Double checked with him since he was older when you and Mom broke up. Even he said he couldn't remember you having any lady friends around. Not even when he lived with you. So either you've been a monk for the last ten years... Which, honestly, is so much better to imagine, because eww. Or, for whatever reason, you didn't want them to meet us."

She pressed her lips together and her shoulders slumped as she glanced down and picked at the blanket when she said the last part. Almost as if her feelings were hurt that I'd not had her around any of the other women.

"Hey, now. It's not that I didn't want them to meet you. After your mom and I divorced my focus was on making sure you two didn't miss my presence being in the house every day. The trips back and forth to see you on the weekends. Or to go to your recitals or your brother's games. My time with you two was just that, my time with you two. I never wanted you to feel like you'd have to compete for my attention."

There was also the fact that I'd refused to confuse them more by having them around a lot of different women. Not that I'd dated all that much, but Porsha and I had agreed that the kids would only meet our new partners if it was a relationship that we'd deemed to be serious.

"And now? Like, she seemed nice, but if she moves in here will she not want me around?"

I slid over and wrapped my arms around her shoulders, tugging her to me. "Listen, you are getting way ahead of yourself. I'm renovating her house, remember? That means she has her own place to live. Secondly, this is your home and always will be. Besides, Cynthia would never do something like that. You and your brother may be older now, but that doesn't change your importance or position in my life."

She wrapped her arms around my waist and squeezed. "Guess it's just weird."

"What is?"

"The idea of you dating. Mom and MJ tried to get me to stay with them, but I like staying here and spending time with you. I worried that would change."

I tightened my hold on her and pressed my lips to the top of her head. "I'm happy to hear you like hanging out with your old man."

"Happy enough to buy me a new car?"

"Oh, I see. All this was to butter me up?" I asked through a laugh.

She sat up and looked at me with her eyes wide and a soft smile. "No, but I figured it couldn't hurt."

I shook my head with a little laugh. "What do you want to do today?"

She untangled herself from the blanket and pushed off the couch. "Mom texted. She wants to get back early so will be here in about an hour."

That news wasn't what I wanted to hear. I liked my time with my daughter, and sadly, the older she got, the less of it we had with all her activities and overly active social calendar. And I knew that time was going to dwindle down even more when she entered college in the fall.

"Hey, Dad," she called from halfway down the hall.

I turned to look over the sofa at her. "Yeah?"

"Are you bringing her to my graduation?"

"I hadn't thought about it."

"Well, you can if you want." With that, she turned and bopped down the hall to her room.

❧ 26 ❧

CYNTHIA

IT WAS ALL TAKING SHAPE. MARCEL SAID WE'D PASSED THE first round of inspections, so today his crew was putting up the drywall and things would move faster from there. The house. My house would no longer be a shell. All the electrical rewiring and plumbing had been completed. The upstairs rooms were set, and my owner's suite was beginning to look like a real place I could live instead of a dusty and somewhat scary attic.

I was really doing this. About to embark on a new journey and run my own business.

And on top of that, I was now having to juggle preparing for a wedding in August. With a location in place, MJ and Olivia finally set a date. I took a sip of my coffee and watched Marcel and Jerry through the kitchen window as they undoubtedly discussed the deck I wanted out at the water's edge. The loungers I'd picked out to go on the platform would be perfect. A nice, quiet place to start the day or maybe end it with a glass of wine.

Marcel. The rollercoaster that was us had me in a loop and upside down. Since the missed dinner he'd been different. Not cold, but more...reserved. Almost as if he had a guard up even though he said he understood the emergency.

I shook my head and turned away. The business needed my focus, as did my friend. Things weren't good, and although she hadn't fired Trent yet, she said he seemed to suspect something was up since she'd restricted his duties. It was all too much, and I simply didn't have the mental capacity for Marcel's mood swings. Even though I'd caused them. I didn't know what we were headed toward, but I was fully aware despite the years that had passed, hurt remained, and that rested with me.

On my way upstairs, I weaved through the workers, who all smiled and waved. Each of the men and women on his crew were great, and I could tell they genuinely enjoyed their work, or more so working for Marcel. They laughed and joked around often. The comradery was evident. Today some of the older kids from his class were onsite learning how to hang drywall.

Despite the ups and downs with us, Marcel was a good man. Not that I should have been surprised by that. It was who he'd always been.

Activity at every corner, except my aunt's room. Not a soul was in there, and when I thought back, I honestly couldn't remember a time when I was here and someone other than Marcel was working in that space. I closed my fingers around my necklace and smiled. Another one of the little things.

"Cynthia!"

Over the banging, sawing, and general talking I heard her voice. I closed my eyes and prayed in vain that she'd just go away.

"Cynthia. I know you here girl," she bellowed again.

Nine weeks. I was surprised it'd taken her this long. I'd known this day would come eventually. I was honestly surprised I'd managed two months strategically crafting my steps to draw out the inevitable. But no amount of wishful thinking or ignoring the reality would change the fact I would have to face my parents. My mother. But her being here... It made my blood run cold. A confrontation. Every conversation with my mother was always a battle.

"Where you at, girl?"

My feet were like lead as I headed down the stairs to see her peeking out from the parlor. There she was, Mary Marshall. Shoulder length hair as black as night from the dye. Face fully made, because a real woman never left the house without her makeup on. Words she'd repeated often, normally in a sneer when I'd do just that.

I kicked my own ass for my constant avoidance of this particular encounter, which unfortunately, brought it to my doorstep. No big surprise my father wasn't with her. He still did cross-country hauls, and I partially believed he refused to retire simply to avoid time with his wife. He surely spent more time on the road than he ever did at home when I was growing up, effectively avoiding us both.

"Hello, Mother."

Her head jerked back like I'd slapped her. "Mother? All that time away turned you even more uppity, huh? Thought you were so good, leaving for college and shit, and where did you end up? Right back where you should have kept your ass all along."

I tried not to wince at her statement. No hello, no nice to see you, and no hugs of excitement. None of that. Instead, I got the same bitter, cutting attitude that she'd dished out my entire childhood. I glanced around. The few workers milling about exchanged curious glances that I didn't want to acknowledge.

"What's all this? What you call yourself doing here? What you doing to my sister's house?"

"It's my house, Mama. And I'm renovating it. Turning it into a B&B."

Unease settled in my stomach. Damn it, why hadn't I just sucked it up and gone to see her? Mary Marshall had no filter and loved being center of attention. Good or bad. And putting me in my place with witnesses around apparently remained her favorite pastime.

Some things never changed.

She cocked a hip out, and her bright red nails stood out against the black fitted pants when she planted her hands on her hips. Her slender legs perched upon the strappy heels she wore. I had to admit, if nothing else, the woman passed on amazing genes. Because no one would believe she was fifty-nine looking at her. My mother was a beautiful woman. And I was nearly her mirror image. However, who we were on the inside couldn't have been more different.

"A what now?"

"It's a bed and breakfast. A more intimate, small scale hotel of sorts."

She closed the distance between us, a frown marring her otherwise impeccable face. "So you can let strangers stay in my sister's house, but turn your back on family? And with your granddaddy in the hospital again, I'm surprised you ain't around to circle the wagon. That's what you did last time, whisking my sister away and not allowing us to care for her."

I took a slow breath. I was not about to get into this again with her. My mother did very little that didn't benefit her. And I knew damn well she didn't have a caring, nurturing bone in her body, so for her to suggest otherwise was downright laughable. Her insinuation about my motives however was very much on brand for her.

They were all pissed off about the will and made sure I knew it. However, I wouldn't be swayed then, and I wasn't about to be swayed now. Auntie had made her choice, and it wasn't like they didn't get something; she wouldn't do that. It was just that none of them felt like they got enough.

"Look, it's busy, and I don't want you hurting yourself with those shoes." I glanced down to prove my point. "I was going to come by to see you and Daddy, we can talk then."

I took her elbow and started to direct her from the house.

She yanked free. "You ain't slick. You took the money and the house then scurried off never to be heard from. Now you back, and showboating, but still act like you too good for us."

"Me? You couldn't be bothered with me for most of my life —" I took a breath. I knew her game, and I wasn't playing.

She loved to start shit, then wanted to play the victim when called on it. She did it with my father, my aunt, and with me. She was never to blame for anything no matter how much she ran her mouth or pushed people's buttons. And she was here to push mine.

"There you go again, acting like you were so mistreated. I did the best I could, but it wasn't good enough for you. Nothing was. That's why you single and childless. Always uppity with high-ass standards."

I couldn't speak. It didn't matter how old I was, her words could cut me like none other. Me wanting a mother who praised her every once in a while. One who offered up hugs and words of comfort equaled "high-ass standards" in my mother's book.

"Mrs. Marshall. It's been too long." Marcel's voice boomed behind me, and I silently thanked his rescue.

On the rare occasions we'd hang out at my house, she'd never failed to a find reason to get on my case, and he'd always known how to break up the tension. Somehow placating her but managing to be on my side while doing so. It was a gift he'd mastered that no one else seemed to. Or cared to. Not even me.

"Ooh, Marcel Lewis. Looking as good as ever," she said pulling him in for a hug. She always knew when to turn on the charm. "See, if you'd known what was good for you, you would have married this man, and had some babies instead of—"

"Instead of what? Getting a college education? Instead of doing something more with my life than chasing after a man that don't want you? There's a reason Daddy stay gone all the time. And this...this right here is why I did, too. You didn't want me, I get it, you made sure I knew it every day of my life. You both did, him being absent as much as humanly possible and you with your very blunt words."

"Girl, hush. You talking 'bout stuff that ain't true. Always whining and moaning. I raised you, took care of you and what thanks did I get?"

"I'm supposed to thank you? You and Daddy being careless

and getting knocked up at sixteen was not my damn fault. You didn't want me here so I left as soon as I could and still, still that didn't make you happy. Nothing does. You didn't want me here, and you didn't want me gone. What you wanted was for me to be stuck like you. Angry and bitter over a life I should have had but didn't because of some unwanted pregnancy? But I got out. I didn't let my life be derailed."

All the noise around seemingly stopped. We stared at each other, neither one of us speaking. And the tingle under my skin over the realization of the words which had poured out with Marcel standing right next to me. She played me like a damn fiddle every time and I let her. No matter how many times I told myself I wouldn't let her drag me in...I always fell for it. My mother was an undertow I couldn't free myself from.

"Cynthia," Marcel started but I waved him off.

"Uh-huh. I can't...I won't do this. Not with her." The moment I looked at him I regretted it. His pain-stricken expression made my heart plummet and bile rise up my throat. "And not with you."

❧ 27 ❧

MARCEL

THE TENSION HAD REMAINED LONG AFTER BOTH CYNTHIA AND her mother had left. The crew would be whispering and stop when I'd walk into the room. Keeping on a brave face was easy when I stayed busy. None of them needed to know how Cynthia's words, words that were meant to be directed at her mother, had cut my soul and left the broken bits scattered in the wind. They didn't know how it even related to me. To us.

And for the first time that I could remember, my instincts weren't to run after her. The emptiness and fresh pain I carried prevented me from wanting to make it better for her. This time I had nothing to give.

I rested my head on the back of my sofa, gripping the quickly warmed and still full beer in my hand. The shower hadn't helped. My stomach churned too much to eat. I could only sit in the quiet calm of my house and replay what she said over and over. A scratched record on repeat.

The ding of my doorbell interrupted the silence. I stayed put, hoping whoever would go away, but the sound came again. Setting my beer down, I pushed off the couch with a heavy sigh. I was not in the mood to entertain anyone, but a peek out my peephole and I knew I'd not be getting rid of my visitor.

"Hey, man," Eddie said, holding up a six-pack.

The small-town gossip network worked fast. And if Eddie was here that meant key words in the exchange between Cynthia and her mom had made it to the right—or wrong—set of ears.

I shut the door behind him. "Jennifer send you, or you heard on your own?"

"JJ came over to hang out with Mark after he got done working with you and they were talking."

Damn, the kids being there on top of the crew. That could be a bigger mess if any of the parents called to complain. JJ was friends with Jennifer and Eddie's oldest, so if he already talked...I scrubbed my hands down my face, yeah phone calls were imminent.

"Look, man, there ain't much I keep from my wife, but what really went down with you and Cyn. You told me that shit in confidence, and to this day I ain't breathed a word. So to hear about today, I had to come check on you."

I don't know why I'd always assumed at some point he let it slip, especially with Cynthia's return. However, I knew my sister, and if she knew, she would have made sure I knew she knew. When Cynthia first left, and I'd exhausted all hopes of getting Regina and Irene to let me know where she was, Eddie was who I'd finally broken down to. I'd needed to tell someone.

I dropped beside him and picked up my bottle, finally taking a long pull.

He popped the top on one for himself. "So, how are you? You two hash out shit? I mean, I almost didn't come cuz I half expected she might be here."

I huffed out a sardonic laugh. "She left. Hopped in her truck and took off leaving both me and her momma standing there. I ain't seen or heard from her and don't 'spect to." I drained the rest of my beer then reached for one out of the pack he brought.

"You ain't call her to check on her? You know her family dysfunctional and shit."

I drank down half the bottle before I spoke. "I'm here. I've always been here. And I just…I just can't. Her choice was her choice, and I don't begrudge her that. But I can't keep chasing a woman that apparently doesn't want to be caught." I finished off the bottle then took both my empty ones to the recycling bin.

She was the one who'd left, that had ended things with next to no explanation. I couldn't make this okay for her. I couldn't shove my feelings aside. Yes, her relationship with her mother had always been rocky, but her words… I couldn't make this okay for Cynthia. Not after what she'd said. Not being her mother meant more to her than anything else. Than anyone else.

Eddie strolled into the kitchen and threw away his bottle. "You know me. Feelings and shit ain't how I normally roll, but what you and Cynthia had was special. Anyone that was around you two could feel it. And with her back, well, it's almost like those missing years made no difference. That whatever it is, is there. I saw it when she came to lunch, in how you seemed to act different. Like the part of you she took when she left was back. You need to handle that."

"Who are you and what the fuck did you do with my friend, because that speech was some body-snatcher-level stuff."

He swatted at the air. "Pish, man whatever, you know what I'm fucking saying. Your sister can be pushy and hella head-strong, and yeah sometimes it's annoying as fuck, but one thing I've learned from that is to communicate. You know I was a moody fuck after my accident."

He paused and scratched at the back of his neck. He'd lost the life he thought he'd have in a blink of an eye. And while our circumstances were totally different, I understood the anger that came along with the adjustment to something new.

"Jen didn't take my shit when she was my nurse, and she sure as hell won't take it now. If I got an issue, I better damn well say what it is and not stew on it and 'stress her the fuck out over nonsense,' in her words."

I laughed and shook my head, knowing he spoke the truth. Mincing words was never my sister's style. There'd been a time

Cynthia and I could and would talk about anything. Unfortunately, we'd been doing a coordinated two-step since her return. Today's untimely events may have brought some of it to light in the heat of the moment, but with her running off, chances of her being willing to talk now were slim to none. And if I was being honest with myself, I didn't know if I was in the right place to deal with it now. The cool-down might be good for us both. One thing was for sure, I needed her to make the first move this time around.

⁂

I WASN'T surprised Cynthia didn't show up at the house the next day. For the most part, the crew was back to normal, no more hushed conversations that stopped when I entered a room. But I also kept to myself as much as possible. The renovation of her aunt's room was my project; I'd told everyone I'd handle it, and they didn't push. Not that I expected them to. Laying the tile in the shower got my full attention and kept me busy so my mind didn't wander too much. It'd done that plenty last night, and I'd tossed and turned until the wee hours of the morning.

There was at least another three to four weeks left on this project before she had the keys and could start her new business. My mark would be on her house. Regardless of how things went with us personally, making it a place she'd be proud of and would do the memory of her aunt justice kept me going. And I hoped that when she walked these halls, when she made breakfast in the newly expanded and updated kitchen, hell, when she curled up on her sofa at the end of the day and stared at the exposed rafters in her unit that maybe, just maybe, she'd think of me. As sappy as all that sounded. And I would never utter a word of it out loud.

My heart was always on my sleeve. I loved her then, and I loved her now. However, it was becoming painfully evident that what I once believed to be a sure thing was anything but.

I stepped back and admired my work. The light blue, glass subway tiles laid in a herringbone pattern looked damn good. She'd splurged, getting the ones that were hand-cut, which provided just the tiniest bit of irregularity but gave that authentic period feel. Her aunt had been an avid bird-watcher, and Cynthia had said the blue color reminded her of a blue jay, her aunt's favorite bird. It was more than fitting for that to be the tile in this room. She didn't know it, but for the shampoo niche, I'd found hand-painted tiles, which, when put together, would show a picture of a blue jay.

Regardless of the shit between us, I wanted to make this place as perfect as I could for her.

28

CYNTHIA

SEVEN DAYS. A FULL WEEK HAD PASSED SINCE MY MOTHER'S visit and my outburst. A full week since words spoken in anger with her had subsequently hurt Marcel in the process.

Hurt him again.

A full week since I'd not been able to close my eyes and not see the expression on his face. It was seared into my damn memory. And a full week since he'd not bothered to reach out to me. I knew in my heart of hearts I had no right to expect him to come fix me, but still I'd hoped.

The fact that he hadn't spoke volumes. The sex. The chemistry between us. Well, that was all easy. But the everything else. We'd been...*I'd* been avoiding what needed to be said, and leave it up to my mother to force it out of me. Though I couldn't blame her...not entirely. There'd been plenty of opportunity to clear the air, and I was admittedly avoiding that hard conversation. For years I'd maintained I had nothing to apologize for. But I'd been wrong.

What was I thinking coming back here?

"Damn, woman, you look like shit," Regina exclaimed when I entered the kitchen.

"Good morning to you, too."

"Sorry, sorry. But you look like I feel most days lately."

She got up from the table and went to pour me a cup of the delicious-smelling coffee. I fixed me a plate of the leftover eggs and sausage before putting a bagel in the toaster.

"Sleep is not my friend."

Regina squeezed my arm and set the cup on the counter. "He hasn't called?"

I shook my head. "The only person blowing up my phone is my mama, demanding an apology for being so 'disrespectful' to her and 'embarrassing' her in front of folks."

Regina rolled her eyes and shook her head. Like most in this town, she knew my mother's antics well. Being the preacher's daughter meant most folks tiptoed around her, but they talked behind her back.

I took a long sip of the hot, bitter liquid and hoped it would warm what I now suspected to be a completely frozen heart. The bagel popped up, and she handed me the butter and cream cheese from the fridge.

"Why don't you call him?"

It was the logical question. A simple question. And something I'd been asking myself every day since. The answer was also simple. I was scared. Anytime I'd thought I'd worked up the nerve, the memory of his pained expression flashed and I'd chicken out. Picking up my plate and mug, I shuffled over to the table.

My stomach churned, but I forced the bite of nearly cold eggs down. "It's easier this way. Can get the house finished, he can go on about his life, and I can do the same with mine."

My friend settled back in her chair and crossed her arms. The pout of her lips and squint of her eyes meant I was in for a lecture.

"Look when you left, I got it. I did. Considering all the shit with your family. I'mma be real, it didn't sit right with how you handled things with Marcel, but you my girl and I had your back. Still do. Which is why I can say, girl, you being ridiculous now."

I blinked slow and stared across the table. The ache in my stomach grew worse. "What you mean it didn't sit right? You and Irene were all in agreement. Now you changing your tune?"

"What the hell else you thought we'd say? You were already facing an impossible and hard decision. We were fucking eighteen and didn't really know shit and were already sad you was leaving to begin with. But what we did know was we would support you because that's what you needed. Wasn't no reason to make things harder by voicing a different opinion." She leaned forward and grasped my hands in hers. "I just felt that at the very least, you should have told him you were leaving. That's all I'm sayin'."

The weight of her words added to the stones in my stomach. Through thick and thin, we'd always supported each other. When I'd needed them most at what should have been the start of our new lives, they'd been there for me. Holding my hand and telling me it would be okay as I'd cried over the fact that after all the fights and declarations I would never be like her, I'd found myself in the same predicament as my mother.

When Regina had lost her husband, both Irene and I dropped everything to come be by her side. We'd helped her through her grief and took on caring for Darnell when she wasn't able. So, to hear the truth of how she really felt about my choice to not tell Marcel when I was leaving, it hit hard. But honestly, it also wasn't surprising. He was as much their friend as he was mine, and knowing how he'd been after I'd gone...her tough love was not the betrayal I wanted it to be.

"You didn't see him, Gina. How am I supposed to face him?"

"Like the grown and sexy woman you are, that's how. Seriously, do you really think you can live here and not see him? Come on, you know better than that. A few trips back and playing 'dodge Marcel' is one thing, but you home, girl. You home."

I gave her hand a tight squeeze before picking up my cooling cup of coffee. I was home and planning to stay. She was right.

Visits were one thing, living here full time was a whole other, no matter how much I wanted to lie to myself otherwise.

"You don't understand, I'm pretty sure what I said killed any and all remaining feelings he might have had for me." I followed up my statement by taking a sip of my drink, hoping the luke-warm liquid would push the lump in my throat down.

"I swear to the lord almighty you can be thick-headed some-times. Do you know how much that man loves you? The moment I told him why I needed his help in getting things started for your aunt's place, you would have thought the gray clouds parted and a ray of sunlight beamed down directly upon him." She accented her exaggerated statement with the wild waving of her hands, which managed to draw a laugh from me.

Her sentiments were over the top, but appreciated. Marcel may have loved me before, but that was a lifetime ago. We were different people now. He'd managed to move on, find love again. Got married and produced a beautiful family.

I loved Marcel with my whole being when we were younger. Being back with him...he'd always made it easy to love him. From the start Marcel had been sweet, and charming, and had a heart of gold. He'd cared. He'd made the effort to show me I was more. More than a mistake. More than a burden. My aunt loved me, but with Marcel, he'd made me feel that I was worthy of being loved. And I didn't want to admit it to myself that over the years, every boyfriend and relationship that came after him had to secretly live up to the standards of care he'd set. Most failed.

Sink or swim, Regina was right, at the very least I owed him the conversation I'd been avoiding for over twenty years.

29

MARCEL

THE SOLACE OF MY SHOP HELPED ME STAY FOCUSED. MY BABY girl had shown up unexpectedly, though part of me believed it was due to the talk from last time. Despite her somewhat acceptance of me dating, I think she still wanted to make sure she had a welcomed place here.

Having her around also provided me with a distraction. We talked about her college choices and I'd scolded her again on her last-minute decision making. She needed to get it together and make a final choice sooner rather than later as her acceptance deadlines were quickly approaching.

Not that I'd ever use her as a shield, but it was damn good to have her around at lunch with Jennifer. It gave my meddling sister someone else to focus on, but she kept throwing me glances. Mary Marshall was well known around town, and not simply due to her father's position, so I had no doubt Jennifer wanted the firsthand account—the multiple messages I'd been ignoring were proof—but refrained from asking because of Alicia.

The sunlight pouring in made me shut down the table saw. I expected to see my daughter standing at the door to tell me she was heading back, but instead, there was Cynthia. I pushed my goggles up to the top of my head and pulled my heavy gloves off.

"When Alicia said workshop, she wasn't kidding," she said, looking around at the various projects in the space.

"Yeah, this detached garage was one of the biggest selling features for me." I leaned against the workbench, folded my arms across my chest, and crossed my ankles.

She gave a smile before shoving her hands into her back pockets. "You know, I never imagined you to do all of this. I mean, you were more into astronomy back in the day, but the pieces you make are stunning."

She ran her hand over the beginnings of a rocking chair I had clamped together. The wonder and pride in her voice warmed my guarded heart.

"Creating calms me. I had anger issues for a while. One of the guys in my unit at Fort Benning got me hooked. His father was a carpenter, and he dabbled. I took to it easily. Now I enjoy seeing something beautiful being transformed from nothing."

She glanced around the space, looking at everything and anything that wasn't me. Not caving and going to her had been hard, but I couldn't. Not this time. However, seeing her now, knowing she was hopefully ready to break the silence, it was just what I needed.

"How long were you in the military?"

"Eight years. I needed to get away because this place wasn't the same after you left. Everything and everyone reminded me of you, so the best escape was to join up. Go anywhere that wasn't here."

I wouldn't sugarcoat things. We'd avoided the subject for long enough. Yes, I wanted us, I wanted the future we'd planned, no matter how delayed it was, but for all my wants, it all rested on her and what she had to say.

She pressed her lips together and dropped her gaze to stare at the shadows dancing across the concrete floor. The only sounds were from the life outside—cars driving, dogs barking, and the low hum of the AC window unit. Everything out there unaware of the silent war raging in these four walls. Seeing her nearly day in and day out for the last couple of months, flirting and falling back into what we were, yet pretending the under-lying tension wasn't there had worn on us both. I wanted answers. I deserved a real explanation, however, I hated how we'd gotten to this point. I hated that an argument with her mother had let the truth I'd known all along come out in such a way.

"What really made you come back? You've avoided this place...me. You've avoided *me* for over twenty years. Why now?"

"Because good or bad, this was my home. And after I lost my job, I realized that ultimately this was where I wanted to live the rest of my days." She took a step forward. "There is something about this place that just feels...right. Every time I came back for a visit, no matter how short, it always felt right. Like my heart knew what my mind refused to process."

I clenched my jaw at the mention of her visits and her two-step around the part where she'd avoided me. I'd know when she was in town, even when she didn't want me to. She'd come and leave under a cloak of secrecy. Much like she'd left initially. Nothing there had changed.

"Why are you here, Cynthia?"

The peace I had been attempting to find was slipping away as we once again evaded the real issue, saying everything yet noth-ing. Bags under her eyes, the slump in her shoulders. Worn down and weary, same as me. I'd spent the last week pushing myself during the day so that when I got home, I'd be bone tired in hopes sleep would come easier. It hadn't.

"I'm sorry. Okay. Can we just move past what I said and—"

"Sorry for what?"

"Excuse me?"

I pushed off the bench, turning to stand so I could face her head on. "What exactly are you sorry for? Leaving? Pretending I didn't exist during those visits you mentioned? Or coming back and upending my life, dredging up old feelings I'd thought I'd put to bed? What are you sorry for, Cynthia?"

She moved so she stood directly in the stream of sun beaming in through the windows. The rays highlighted her golden-brown eyes as they widened at my question. I'd tried to let it go. I tried to tell myself it was in the past, we were starting something new, but I couldn't. I needed to understand more than what she'd written to me. I needed to hear her speak why she didn't love me enough to tell me in person. Why she had to do it the way she had. My soul wouldn't be at peace until that happened, and there was no way in hell we could even attempt anything new with the ghosts of the past haunting us.

"I didn't come here to argue with, Marcel."

"Then why did you come? Do you even fucking know? Or is it more convenient to make everything have a double meaning so that nothing is ever fucking resolved? Maybe you need absolution. You want me to say I forgive you without you so much as acknowledging how I fucking felt."

I tried to keep my voice low. I didn't want Alicia to hear, or the neighbors. Keeping my business out of the gossip mill was a never-ending endeavor.

"We were great together, Cyn. I would have moved heaven and earth for you. And you just threw it all away. And for what?" The anger, frustration, and, ultimately, the sadness I thought I'd made peace with came roaring back as if it were yesterday, not two decades ago.

"I didn't throw anything away, Marcel. I lived the life I wanted. I needed out. I couldn't stay trapped here."

"Trapped? Marrying me and possibly raising a family would have trapped you? I would have never stopped you from exploring your dreams. You just didn't give us a chance. Me a chance to figure out how to make it work."

"Make what work? Me forgoing my scholarship to maybe go to some community college instead, if even that? I was *not* going to be her. Forced into a life I didn't want. Angry, bitter, and unhappy. I was not going to have a child grow up like that. Unwanted and resented," she cried.

My stomach clenched, and my chest ached at her admission. Unwanted and resented. The terse relationship with her parents was no secret. It colored a lot of her life outlooks, but we were different. What we had was different. Or at least I'd thought so.

I stared at her, watching as she angrily wiped the tears away only for them to be replaced with fresh ones.

"You're not her. And I'm sure as hell not him. You didn't have to leave the way you did, Cynthia." I poked at my chest. "You left me like I meant nothing. Like the years we'd had meant nothing."

"It wasn't about you. You can hate me all you want for doing it, but it wasn't about you. Can't you see that? It was me. I had to do it for me, or I wouldn't have been able...if my parents or grandparents... Leaving, it was my only option."

I stormed toward her, stopping just before reaching where she stood. "Bullshit. It wasn't your only option. It was fucking cowardly. And the worst part..." I stopped as the memories ripped through me. "I never hated you, Cyn. It was never about the fact you had the abortion. You left. I would have...I wanted to be there for you. I should have been allowed to be there for you. It was never about your choice, it was always about how you handled it. Then after everything, you mailed me some bullshit letter and ghosted me for twenty fucking years. We deserved better than that." My chest rose and fell in controlled breaths. I stepped closer, erasing more of the physical space between us, but the canyon-sized divide remained. "I deserved better than that."

She took in a deep, shuddering breath then collapsed against me.

30

CYNTHIA

MARCEL WRAPPED HIS ARMS AROUND ME AND RESTED HIS CHIN on my head. He was right. The day I'd told him I was pregnant and uttered the words I can't have it, his only response was to hold me and whisper, "Okay." I knew he'd never try to sway me or guilt me for my decision. I knew he'd do exactly what he'd always done and that was precisely why I'd had to leave.

"If you'd been there…I couldn't have you there, Marcel. I never wanted to hate you, and if you'd been there, I don't know if I could have done it, and I would have hated you for it."

He took in a deep breath but said nothing. I'd never regretted my choice to abort. The moment the test turned positive it was my first and only thought. And it was easier to not let myself worry about how that would make him feel. Or at least that was the lie I'd told myself when the hard truth was I'd spent the last twenty-plus years doing my damnedest to avoid him so I wouldn't be faced with this: having to speak my truth and possibly see the love he had for me drain from his eyes in real time.

"And after?" his deep baritone voice rumbled, and I closed my eyes before pulling away.

"And after…you already called it. I was being a coward." I

swiped at the tears on my cheeks and gazed deep into his dark, brown, sad eyes. "There are few people in this world I'm scared to disappoint. You matter, Marcel. You have always mattered to me."

I closed my fingers around the cross hanging around my neck. Telling my aunt, especially with her own history and struggles, had been harder than telling Marcel. She'd been the amazing woman she'd always been. We talked at her kitchen table over bowls of melting ice cream. No judgment, only support.

The same thing I would have gotten from Marcel, but having them both there...it would have been too much. Another choice had to be made, and her words echoed in my ear: "Don't be scared, Cynthia." Those words were about more than what I was planning to do. They were about living life on my terms, good or bad. Even if that meant breaking the heart of the man I loved in the process. Breaking my own heart.

I placed my palms on his chest, the warmth from his body seeped through my skin. "You would have been sweet and caring. You would have been you. Hell, you even said as much. You would have moved heaven and earth to make me happy... and in doing so would have given up your own hopes and dreams."

He lowered his head and wrapped his fingers around my wrists, ever so softly stroking my flesh with his thumb, unable to refute my truth. He'd wanted kids, the picket fence life and I... didn't.

"You have two wonderful children. They are beautiful and kind and funny. If I hadn't left...if I'd stayed, if I'd stayed with you...eventually, you would have resented me. Yes, it'd scared me to think I'd get to a point in my life where I could resent you and the life we would have had. But the biggest terror, the one that plagued me most, was for you to feel that way about me. If the love you'd had for me had morphed into anything else, if I'd been faced once again with the attitude and general disinterest I'd gotten from my parents, that would have killed me more than I can articulate."

I pressed my lips together and steadied myself before continuing. "I was wrong in how I handled things. I admit that. And, god, I'm sorry. I truly am. But I don't regret not having the baby. Having our baby. I loved you. I love you...but that... And seeing where we are now, you can't tell me it wasn't the right thing to do."

I reached up to cup his face. "You did deserve better. You deserved to have everything you'd ever wanted in life. You deserved more than I would have been able to give you. I was freeing you as much as I was freeing myself."

I let out a long and slow exhale. Saying the words. No longer hiding behind the fear and worry. Putting the truth out between us, the weight I'd carried since the night I'd left disintegrated.

Marcel snaked his hands around my waist. He did a slow opening then closing of his fingers along my sides. Gazing into his eyes, the torment remained, but also an acceptance.

"I wish you'd told me. Been honest. I'm not saying I would have completely understood then, the thought of losing you...but I just wish I'd been given the chance."

"I know."

He took another deep breath. "It hurt, you leaving like you did. I was angry and heartbroken...but...I love my children. What they've brought into my life, having them...I wouldn't trade that for anything. Not even to replace the pain I had over your departure." A melancholy smile graced his face. He stroked his thumb along my cheek. "I wouldn't have wanted resentment to form between us either."

There were times when love wasn't enough, and our different wants from life were one of them. We wouldn't have lasted back then because in order for one of us to be happy, the other wouldn't have, and that would have been no way to live.

But this moment, as we stood together realizing that truth, I knew our relationship was strong, and like the house he was renovating for me, it had good bones. It just needed to have some walls knocked down. A few things rearranged for it to be the best it could be.

I tilted my head up and pressed my lips to his. The kiss started slow, but the grip on my shirt tightened and he tugged my body closer. He pushed his tongue forward, invading my mouth. I moaned against him, wrapping my arms around his neck. He devoured me with urgency and renewed passion. My head spun, and my body tingled.

He broke from the kiss and trailed his nose along my jawline while pushing his calloused fingers under my shirt. The tickle of his beard acted as a seduction in itself. I wanted and needed him like never before. When I managed to get my hand between our bodies and grip his erection, his low groan was like a siren's call to my own arousal. Marcel stepped back, and with hooded eyes and his mouth slightly open, he kept caressing me. A slow open then close of his fingers as I stroked him through his pants.

He glanced over his shoulders, and my attention followed his line of sight. Against the far wall near the AC unit was a wooden bench with a plush but worn leather seat. I nodded my understanding before a moment of panic hit, causing me to turn toward the door.

He leaned down to kiss the side of my neck as he raised my shirt higher until he palmed my breasts and stroked my pebbled nipples through the thin fabric. "Don't worry," he murmured. "She rarely comes out here. But..." He walked over and locked it all the same.

As he strolled back toward me, slow and steady, the devilish grin on his face and the lust in his eyes, the energy radiating from him stole my breath and dampened my panties. My knees went weak. There was no longer a storm cloud hanging over us, and when his lips once again covered mine, I surrendered. The kiss was comfort and familiarity, but also new and fresh. The kiss was freedom and understanding. The kiss was our new beginning.

"I've missed you," he whispered, grabbing my ass with both hands.

I clung to his back and pressed closer to his hardened erection. "I've missed you, too."

Marcel walked us backward to the bench, kissing and touching every part of me he could.

A primal need took over. An urgency to connect. To commit on a new level. On a level of open honesty that now tethered us together.

I toed off my Keds, the coolness of the concrete floor seeped through my socks. I unbuttoned my shorts. "Condoms?"

He pushed his pants down and sat on the bench. His erection stood tall and ready. I licked my lips, recalling the addictive taste and feel of him in my mouth.

"In the house. But I've had a vasectomy." He stretched his hand out to me. "And before you, it'd been a good year or more since I've been with anyone."

"Same. Well, not the vasectomy part," I added with a wink.

I slipped my hand in his, and the spark when our skin touched zinged through me. As I straddled him, as our bodies melded into one, our gazes remained locked. I lowered down, reveling in the glorious stretching of my body so willing and able to accept all he had to offer. I knew I was home. That he was home. From the moment I'd left, I was no longer whole. I'd survived, I'd lived, but there was always a shadow.

Marcel burned away that darkness. The way he could make everything better with a look or a touch. His constant love and support. I wanted nothing more than to get lost in him.

He reached under my shirt, pushing my bra up, and the coarseness of his calloused hands on my breast was nothing short of marvelous. Marcel lifted it to his mouth, sucking on the hardened nipple, his tongue swirling around and sending shockwaves along my nerve endings. I held on to his broad shoulders, pumping my hips along his shaft.

Home.

Not a place. Not a house.

Him.

"That's it, baby. Take what you need," he grunted. He thrust up, matching my moves. The angle perfection, hitting the hidden bundle of nerves and bringing me closer and closer to my end.

He held my ass, grabbing and squeezing my flesh, aiding in my movements.

I wrapped my arms around his neck and kissed him again, the need to have every connection possible driving me. The soft rubbing of my clit along his stomach was the extra sensation needed to push me spiraling into an abyss of pleasure. I buried my face in his neck to muffle the noise as I cried out.

He gripped me and held me close while letting out a long groan, spilling his release into me.

I rested my head on his shoulder as we both tried to catch our breaths.

"I'm sorry," I whispered.

"For what?"

"Leaving you."

He wrapped his arms around me and held tight. "Don't do it again."

I sat up and looked at him. I placed my hands on either side of his face and kissed him softly. "I wouldn't make the same mistake twice."

❧ 31 ❧

MARCEL

THE PAINTERS WERE HARD AT WORK ON THE EXTERIOR. Cynthia wanted to keep the color palette original to what it had been, so a creamy white with light blue trim. The shutters had all been repaired, the front porch was swing ready. The outside was coming along nicely. We had maybe another couple of weeks' worth of work before The Blue Bird Inn was ready to receive its first guests.

"One day I guess I'll be able to stand around and just watch everyone work," MJ said as he jogged down the stairs, large grin on his face.

"Perks of being the boss."

"Yeah, yeah, yeah. Don't forget, boss, that we have to be in Savannah in the morning to meet with our potential new client. You're going to love it, they want modern everything."

I ran my hand over my head and groaned. While I appreciated the referral work, the modern style wasn't my favorite, but for business I'd suck it up with a smile.

"I think you agree to these things just because you get to take the lead."

He tapped the side of his forehead. "All part of my master plan for a hostile takeover of the family business."

I barked out a laugh then pulled him in for a hug, which he easily returned. "Good luck with that." I tightened my arms around him before letting go. "I love you, and I am so proud of you."

"Love you, too, old man."

I shoved him a little. Him and his sister loved the "old man" title. And they knew they could only get away with that with me because their mother would not entertain such a thing, even in playing.

Cynthia had been right. I'd always known my life would need to involve children, and hers not so much. For either of us to have to compromise on something so major would have possibly led to the resentment she'd feared. The way she'd gone about things hurt, and if there could have been a do-over I would have loved that, but the past couldn't be changed. And holding on to what should have been did no one any good.

She didn't regret not having our child. And surprisingly the fact didn't hurt as much as I'd thought it would. She'd lived the life she'd wanted, and I'd done the same. And had two amazing children to show for it. People I'd nurtured, loved, and couldn't imagine not having in my life. It was a twenty-five-year detour, but now our lives were back on the same path.

"When are you going to tell Ms. Spoiled Rotten she's getting a new car?"

"She's spoiled? I'm pretty sure you both will drive me into the poor house." I gave him a pointed look, and he threw his hands up in mock surrender. The house he and Olivia called home was made possible because Porsha and I had given them the down payment.

Being able to provide for my kids was my greatest joy. And I worked my ass off to make sure they never had to go without. Probably more because for the longest time I carried guilt over the divorce, no matter how mutual and friendly it had been.

"Tomorrow. She's coming down this evening. I told her we'd

take her old car to get an estimate on a paint job, but we will really head to the dealership where it'll be waiting with a bow."

He laughed as he took off his hard hat and ran his arm across his forehead before replacing the protective gear. "She's been so annoyed having to drive her car with the mismatched bumper. Be sure to wear ear plugs because she's going to scream like crazy."

"Good point. I'll be sure to pack some."

He turned his attention to the house. "It's going to look great when finished."

"Yeah, it is. I'm making two rocking chairs for one side of the porch, and there will be a swing on the other. Speaking of making things, when are you coming over to help with the arch?"

It warmed my heart to see his face light up. My boy was getting married, and for him to be doing so at a place that held so many good memories and I had a connection to upped the ante. I knew the day wasn't about me, but it still added to the overall pride and joy for the upcoming event.

"Next Sunday? We can make a day of it, get the smoker going early with some ribs, maybe a brisket. Let 'em cook while we work."

"What I'm hearing is, in order for me to get you to do some work, I need to feed you."

Once again, a full smile spread across his face. "I'll bring the beer."

"Deal. And don't forget, dinner at my house tonight."

"You know I never pass up a free meal. Livie and I will be there with bells on."

He did a small salute before he walked back into the house. A sense of contentment settled over me. My kids were happy. Cynthia and I were starting over. And I was part of the new life and business she was building. I grabbed my hardhat from the hood of my truck and headed in behind him. Outside of my own house, never had a project been so important to me.

THE SIGHT of Cynthia's 4Runner in my driveway brought a giant grin to my face. She'd been serious about wanting to make up the missed dinner, and her being genuinely interested in getting to know not only Alicia, but also Olivia better...words couldn't describe how ecstatic that made me.

What I found when I opened my door seemed so natural. Cynthia at the stove with soft jazz playing through my Bluetooth speakers.

She turned and smiled. "Hey."

I strolled over and wrapped my arms around her waist from behind and placed a kiss on her shoulder. "Hey yourself. It smells damn good in here."

She reached back and stroked my cheek. "We're having baked chicken, mashed potatoes, green beans, and cornbread."

I whistled through my teeth. "A man could get used to this."

She turned in my arms and tilted her head to the side. "What? Me cooking for you?"

I shook my head and tightened my hold on her. "Just you being here."

A smile stretched across her face. "Go shower. Wouldn't want your daughter to walk in on you pawing at the new woman in your life."

I eased my hands down to grab her ass. "You mean like that?" I asked, pressing my lips to the side of her neck.

"Yeah...like that."

A car door slamming got our attention. I stole a quick kiss from Cynthia before heading over to the door to greet Alicia.

"Hey, baby girl. How was the drive?"

"Easy and uneventful like always," she replied with a slight rolling of her eyes. She handed me her overnight bag then walked over to Cynthia and gave her a quick hug. "Dinner smells good, Ms. Cynthia."

"Thank you. Should be done shortly."

"You need any help?"

I eased out of the kitchen and left the two of them talking. After dropping Alicia's bag in her room, I ducked into mine and stopped at the sight of the small suitcase parked at the foot of my bed. Cynthia was planning to stay the night. We'd planned this dinner, she'd been uneasy about possibly taking time away from Alicia, but I'd reminded her that being part of my life meant being part of theirs. Plus, I'd been serious about liking the idea of coming home to her. Wherever home may be. That was something we could work out later.

Laughter filtered down the hall as I headed toward the kitchen after my quick shower. Cynthia standing there, smiling and talking with my children squeezed my heart in the best possible way. Over dinner, the conversation flowed easily from the final stages of construction on the house, to Alicia's graduation, and wedding plan talk.

"Dinner was delicious," Alicia commented, pushing her empty plate away from her. She rested her elbows on the table and propped her face on her hands. "Ms. Cynthia have you done any traveling?"

MJ groaned and Olivia let out a small laugh. Alicia had been extremely vocal in her displeasure over her brother's choice of honeymoon destination. She didn't see how a cabin in the mountains of Asheville could be exciting.

"Yeah. It's one of my favorite things to do. I've been to some amazing places and looking forward to seeing more."

My daughter's face lit up. Like Cynthia, Alicia had a bit of wanderlust, and while we'd taken smaller family vacations to Disney, the beach, things like that, going abroad was something she dreamed about.

"What is the most exciting place you've visited so far?"

"Dubai," Cynthia answered without any hesitation. "The trip was a birthday gift to myself, and I loved every minute. The food, architecture, the nightlife, and just the overall opulence was like none other."

As she spoke, a soft smile played on Cynthia's lips. She absolutely came alive as she relayed stories about her travels, both alone and trips with her friends, and the entire time, my baby girl ate it up with enthusiastic attention. I'd never had that same drive to see the world. Moving around with the Army had been enough for me, but witnessing Cynthia discuss what she loved and enjoyed, I suddenly wanted to go anywhere and everywhere with her.

"So, do you think I could tagalong on your next trip?" Alicia asked, hopefulness laced with each word.

Cynthia glanced over at me and grabbed my hand. "Well, I won't be going anywhere anytime soon. Too much going on right now, which means I need to stay planted in Madison. But, as long as your parents agree, you can happily join me on my next trip. I've been thinking about going to the Maldives."

Alicia turned her excited and expectant gaze on me. "Can I?"

"I have to discuss with your mother. But I doubt she'd have a problem, especially if I was also going."

The answer satisfied Alicia, mostly. She did grumble about me crashing "girl time." By the end of the night Olivia and MJ were discussing possible places they could go as a celebration once Olivia graduated.

I held my hand out toward Cynthia as she exited the master bath. "You don't mind me crashing the trip, do you?"

"Not at all."

I wrapped my arms around her. "Is it wrong of me to say I'm glad you got fired?"

She rolled her eyes and settled against me. "Yes, a little. But I'm kinda glad as well." She pressed her lips to the base of my neck. "This is where I belong."

CYNTHIA

The bell above the door chimed as I entered Just A Bit of Sugar. No matter the time of day, there were always people about. Since Marcel had forbidden me from going by the house until it was done, I'd taken to stopping in to lend a hand at the bakery when I could. Regina had said Trent must have sensed something was up because he'd conveniently cashed in his vacation time and would be gone for three weeks.

I hated that my friend had to deal with such a betrayal, and even though she tried to hide it, she shouldered a lot of guilt. I'd told her plenty of times she couldn't blame herself for trusting a person that had been with her for so long.

Mama Charles came from the kitchen and smiled briefly when she saw me, but it quickly turned to the stern look she'd give when a lecture was about to happen. She headed over and filled two ceramic mugs with coffee while I claimed a two-seater table near the back.

"What did I do this time?" I asked with a smile when she set the cup in front of me.

"See, that's the guilt already talking if you asking that question," she replied as she settled into the chair across from me.

"Guilt for what?"

She took her time pouring cream into her coffee then slowly stirred it before answering. The entire time she kept her focus on me. "You been to see your granddaddy?"

I sighed and my shoulders dropped. I hadn't, and she knew I hadn't. Regina had told me he'd been released from the hospital, a message she'd been directed to deliver from the mother figure sitting across from me.

"Look, forgiveness, when and if it happens, no one can rush that. But you need to at least say goodbye and make some sort of peace while you can."

Where my grandfather was concerned, there wasn't really a forgiveness that needed to happen. He was strict in his beliefs, and judgmental of any life choices that went against them, that I knew. I didn't have to forgive him for who he was, I'd simply removed myself from being one of his potential targets. Image had been everything. He was a "good man", a "moral man", and had the town's respect—mine didn't matter.

"I made peace a long time ago, Mama Charles."

She reached across the table and grabbed my hand. "You back now, Cyn. Do you really think you'll be able to live in this town and not interact with your folks?"

"Well, Daddy makes it easy by avoidin' us."

She pursed her lips and settled back in her chair. "That he does."

"I've tried, Mama Charles. I have. But me and her are oil and water. Nothing will ever be enough for her. I've spent too much of my life attempting to make up for simply being born."

"Well," she stopped with a dramatic pause, smacking her lips a few times. "Your momma has her issues, Cyn-Cyn, but I haveta believe that somewhere in her heart she does love and care about you. She just don't know how to show it."

I rolled my eyes heavenward and took in a long breath. I knew Mama Charles meant well, but sadly, she had more faith in

Mary Marshall than I did. The only person my mother knew how to love was herself.

"I can't give her any more of my energy."

I'd spent too many years trying to please a woman that couldn't be sated. She was a succubus of emotion and needed to be the center of everyone's universe. Mama Charles squeezed my hand before letting it go.

"I'll go see him. I promise."

She smiled and pushed away from the table. "Glad you're back." She glanced toward the double steel swinging doors. "I think my girl would be even more of a mess over all this BS with Trent if she didn't have you to lean on."

Her smile faded, and the weariness of the situation showed for a brief moment. I knew Regina felt she carried most of the responsibility, but it was a family matter and they'd all rallied. As I finished my coffee, I fired off a text to Marcel. Going to see my grandfather with the chance my mother might be there was something I didn't want to do on my own.

❧

STANDING in front of the light blue simple bungalow had my stomach in my throat and my heart in competition with the Indy 500. The sight of my mother's car had me wanting to get back in Marcel's truck and hightail it back to his place. He wrapped his warm hand around mine, intertwining our fingers. Facing her would be bad enough, but the idea of the sickness and near death that waited on the other side of the door pulled all the painful memories of my aunt near the end back to the forefront of my mind.

"I'm with you." He brought our joined hands to his lips and pressed a kiss to the back of mine. "You're here for him, not her."

His deep voice and caring eyes were exactly what I needed.

He'd worked all day and only took time to shower before coming to pick me up for this field trip. My legs were like lead as we headed up the three steps to the porch. The flower boxes that my grandmother had always took pride in now sat empty. Chipping paint and warped planks of wood were a stark contrast to the once impeccably up-kept home. Pride and image had been his identity in all things.

Marcel started to ring the bell when the door flew open and I came face to face with the last person I'd expected to find at my grandfather's.

Black and gray stubble lined his jaw. His near white bushy brows were pulled together in the oh so familiar grimace of annoyance that seemed to be ever present. The decades of trucking showed on his face in deep lines around his eyes and buried across his forehead. And even with his somewhat slumped posture now, he still stood tall and imposing. His increased bulk made his already near intimidating stature more intense.

"Daddy."

He stepped back, looked me up and down, then cast a quick glance in Marcel's direction.

"Well, look who we have here. Your momma had said you were back. Goin' on and on 'bout you tearing up Drea's place." He hesitated for just long enough before he leaned in for an awkward and forced hug. "Come 'ere. It's good to see ya." The greeting rang as false as his attempt at physical affection.

"I didn't expect you here."

That was a massive understatement. There was no love lost between the man I'd come to visit and the one standing before me. But when one used his position to force the other into a marriage, the only result would be an acrimonious relationship. So for him to be here...

He tapped the cigarette in his hand on the top of the pack before putting it between his lips to light it up. After a long draw, he blew the horrid-smelling smoke out the side of his mouth and glanced back over his shoulder. "Yeah, well, your momma's been bitchin' that I needed to be here in her time of need."

The aloofness and disinterest were clear as he took another drag of his cigarette. It was the same detachment that made him pause before doing the fatherly thing and hugging his only child —at least as far as I knew—whom he hadn't seen in years.

Once again, he blew the smoke up and away and it mingled with another scent reminiscent of him—motor oil. A smell that had seemed to linger in the house long after he'd come and gone for what amounted to a small pit stop.

"Well, you'll find her in the back bedroom holdin' vigil at his side." He nodded in Marcel's direction. "Good seeing ya." He turned his attention back to me. "Tell ya momma I had to run to the sto'. With you here she shouldn't be breathin' down my neck for five minutes."

No additional goodbye hug, or acknowledgment. Instead, Ernest Marshall shouldered past us and ambled down the steps over to Mom's car.

"That man hasn't changed a bit," Marcel said, sliding his arm around my waist. "You okay?"

I leaned into him and rested against his chest. I inhaled deeply, ridding myself of any remnants of the man who'd just left and replacing it with the one I couldn't have done this without. Smoke and motor oil erased by cedar and Irish Spring.

"Do you have wine at your place?"

"We can pick some up on the way home."

Home. I liked the sound of that.

One more fortifying breath, and I stepped over the threshold. I walked into a time capsule. Nothing had changed. The two Tiffany-style lamps cast a dull and almost eerie glow on the small living room. A few voices filtered from the kitchen, probably the owners of the other cars and no doubt some of the church ladies bringing casseroles and being good members of the congregation. And providing my mother with an audience.

I pressed my finger to my lips and hoped we could make it down the creaky hallway without alerting them to our presence. I just wanted to get in and get out. I knew it wouldn't work and two steps in we were stopped to make the obligatory greetings. Smiling, politely nodding as they talked, and of course, the question on why they hadn't seen us on Sunday. Nothing much had changed. And while they were saying they would get on with their evenings to give the family some time, I knew they'd stick around for the chance at having some good gossip. If my parents had been together for any length of time, they probably had plenty; that particular well never seemed to run dry.

The time capsule continued when I stepped into my grandfather's room. Same furniture since my childhood. He lay in the bed, looking weaker than I ever imagined. I gripped Marcel's hand, and the squeeze I got in return was exactly what I needed. Thin and fragile were words I would have never used to describe the patriarch of the family, but they described the man I couldn't take my eyes off of.

"Well, well. Look what the cat drug in." My mother put down the magazine she'd been flipping through and pushed herself up from the chair.

She went about making a fuss, adjusting covers that didn't need adjusting and filling a water cup he probably wouldn't be drinking from.

"Hello, Mrs. Marshall."

She grinned wide and wrapped her arms around Marcel's neck. "Thank you for coming. And for getting her to do the right thing."

I swallowed the retort burning on the tip of my tongue.

He chuckled and shook his head. "I'm here because Cynthia asked me to come." His clear statement of defense was accompanied by him placing his hand on my lower back.

She turned her lip up. "You gon' whisk him away, too, and keep the rest of us from sayin' a proper goodbye?"

I did a slow inhale and exhale. "Momma, can you not do this?"

"Do what, Cynthia?" Her voice rose. "You act like I'm not supposed to be upset I'm losing my last remaining parent. Just because *some* people throw away family if they don't suit their needs don't mean we all do."

She glared at me, daring me to challenge. Hoping I'd challenge. The added inflection in her tone. The glassy eyes as she cued up the crocodile tears. I was not going to let her drag me into another verbal sparring match.

I pinched the bridge of my nose and slowly exhaled. "I'm here to see my grandfather. You can either let me do that now, or I will come back when you're not around. What I'm not going to do is continue to feed into this"—I gestured between the two of us—"any longer."

She opened her mouth to speak, but Marcel spoke first.

"Mary."

Even I startled. One word. Her name, and only her name. She glanced at me, him, back at my grandfather, and back to me.

She squared her shoulders and lifted her chin. "I could use a bite to eat."

She exited the room with all the air of an aristocrat.

"Do you want me to stay with you?"

I shook my head. "Go sit with her as she weaves her tale of woe."

The smile on his face acted as a warm blanket. Marcel leaned and planted a soft kiss on my lips.

"Might need more than a bottle after this." He glanced over at the sick man, who lay unmoving in the bed. "I'll be down the hall."

I took the seat my mother had vacated. As I held my grandfather's hand with its paper-thin skin, I again realized I had more in common with my mother than I wanted to admit. This man had lived with impossible standards set for those around him. Praise directed at either of his daughters had rarely passed his lips.

My mother had sought that validation. And as loathe as I was to acknowledge, part of me still did the same with her and my father. But I couldn't any longer. She was who she was, and I had to accept it. We'd be ships passing in the night around town, and I was okay with that.

MARCEL

I SET THE BOX OF WINES ON THE TABLE ALONG WITH THE BAG containing newly purchased wine glasses and an opener. I was more a beer or bourbon man, but if Cynthia wanted wine, I'd keep it stocked as often as possible.

"You want the red or white?"

"Brown."

I was about to ask her what the hell that was when she wrapped her arms around my waist.

I embraced her and held tight. "Brown it is."

We stood in the middle of my kitchen not speaking. The visit with her grandfather had been more draining than she wanted to let on. It'd been bad enough to have to see him like he was, but adding the stress of both her parents to the mix took a toll.

She slipped her hands under my shirt and glided them up my back, softly gripping and massaging as she went. "You loved me," she whispered.

"I *love* you," I softly corrected.

Cynthia took a deep breath while her fingers continued their hypnotic motion against my skin.

"Back then. For all the craziness and instability. For all the searching for an acceptance that was never going to come. When I thought I was the problem because of how they were...how they are."

She tilted her head back, her eyes were glossy, but the look on her face serene. I leaned and pressed my lips to hers. She dug her fingers into my flesh and allowed my tongue entry into her mouth. Mine twirled around hers, a gentle, slow dance. The act of intimacy comforting and solidifying our commitment to each other.

When we broke apart, what I knew I needed to do more than anything was make love to the woman who'd stolen my heart when she was thirteen. Even when she'd broken it, a piece had remained hers and hers alone. I held her hand and led her out of the kitchen, down the hall to my room. Once inside, I cupped her face and placed a soft kiss on one cheek, then the other, before planting a brief one on her lips.

"I love you," I whispered.

"I love you, too."

I curled my fingers around the hem of her dress, and Cynthia raised her arms to aid in its removal. Tonight, she'd feel my love in every kiss, every touch, every breath that passed my lips. I moved behind her and unhooked her bra. A kiss to her shoulder before I slid the strap down, and a repeat action to the other side. The light green material fell to the floor, joining her discarded dress. My erection ached against the stiff denim of my jeans.

Starting at her stomach, I slid my hands up until the weight of her breasts rested in them. Cynthia moaned low, reaching back to drape an arm around my neck as she leaned against me. I rolled the stiff peaks between my thumb and forefinger. She arched into my touch. My need to see every inch of her delectable body burned through me.

I moved my hands south until one cupped her sex. Her arousal had dampened her panties and made my dick harden more. Tonight, I would get lost in this woman. My woman. As if it was the first time and the last time. I would make love to every inch of her. Slowly, I peeled the remaining fabric down, and she wiggled her legs to help gravity do its job.

She spun in my arms, and our lips connected again as she worked to push my shirt up. There was urgency in her movements, but I wouldn't give in. We tumbled onto my bed, lips locked, and hands roaming.

I ran my nose along her cheek and nipped her ear. Down her neck, across her collarbone. I circled my tongue in the small divot at the base of her neck. With her fingertips, she stroked up and down my arms. It was as if we both needed the connection, to have any parts of our bodies touching.

Time no longer mattered. Only her. As I trailed kisses down her arm, Cynthia was the center of my universe. I brought her hand to my mouth and took care to give each individual digit my undivided attention. Every sigh and soft whimper made me want to go slower.

I eased down her body, licking and nipping at her flesh as I went. When I teased the inside of her thighs with my fingers, she widened her legs. An invitation that was hard to ignore. But not yet.

She rubbed the top of my head, squirming when I licked the skin just below her navel. I lifted her leg and placed a kiss on the inside of her ankle. Slowly, I made my way up her leg, running my nose along her smooth skin. The soft flesh behind her knee. The sweet spot on her inner thigh. Our gazes met when I made it to her hip bone. She grabbed my face, and I gave in to her subtle request.

I settled between her legs, my dick poised at her entrance. Intertwining our fingers, I pushed in, slow and easy. Inch by inch, her slick body welcomed me. Her tongue rolled along her bottom lip beckoning me for another kiss. Our bodies worked in sync, pelvis to pelvis, she rocked her hips up as I pushed forward. Cynthia tightened then relaxed her fingers while our tongues swirled around the other. She widened her legs and planted her feet into the mattress, pushing up looking for more.

Slow and steady, in and out as I relished in the reconnection. Her hot bursts of air that hit my cheek. The quiet whimpers turned to moans. Her lips parted, and breath came out in shallow pants. Cynthia tightened her grip, arched her back, and closed her eyes.

"Open them, baby. I want to see you come," I huffed out between thrusts.

Forehead to forehead, our gazes remained locked as we climaxed together.

✻ 34 ✻

CYNTHIA

AS I TURNED DOWN THE STREET LEADING TO MY HOUSE, nerves had my heart rate going a mile a minute and my stomach churning. Even though Marcel had said the renovations weren't like on TV the first day of the project, he wanted to do a big reveal all the same. Staying away these few weeks had been hard, but I managed for him. He wanted to surprise me, and I wanted him to have the joy of doing so.

So much went through my head replaying how far we'd come. I'd spent nearly every night with him. Attended the first large family event with Alicia's graduation. Porsha's husband was a great guy, but it was still a bit unreal to watch how well they all interacted. And how easily I'd been accepted into the fold. Even his parents were welcoming after everything that had happened. My relationship with my parents might never mend, but I was thankful I'd returned to Madison all the same.

At the end of the drive, Marcel came into view. In dark jeans and another impossibly white shirt, he stood leaning against a post. One that hadn't been there on my last visit. My mouth went dry and my hands shook as I eased my truck to a stop. He strolled over and opened my door, large, sexy grin firmly in place.

"Welcome to The Blue Bird Inn."

Hearing those words made it all real. The months of construction...my dream was now a reality. I slipped my hand into his awaiting one and drew in a slow breath. He led me over to the sign and all the air left my body. The name, the one I'd thought over for a long time because I wanted something that was meaningful and represented my aunt, was carved into the white wood in a beautiful script font. The dark blue paint made it stand out. I stepped closer and reached out to trace over the lettering.

Above the name were two blue jays, hand painted, and depicted to be holding a banner between them that had the year established written on it. I closed my fingers around the cross at my neck. Marcel stepped up behind me and I leaned into him. His quiet strength and support wrapped around me.

"You made this?"

"Yes, one of my special projects."

I swiveled in his arms and looked up. "One?"

"Yes. You already know the wedding arch will be a permanent fixture, but I may have another surprise or two for my favorite client."

I pressed my hands to his cheeks and stretched up to kiss him. Slow and tender, our mouths worked in unison.

"I love you," I whispered against his lips.

"Love you, too," he answered back before pulling away. From his back pocket, he produced a blindfold.

I arched a brow. "We getting kinky in the driveway?"

A sexy smirk quirked one side of his mouth up as he placed the black fabric over my head. "No, but we can certainly put this to use again tonight."

"I'll hold you to that."

His playful wink was the last thing I saw before he slid the cloth over my eyes. With great care, he helped me into my truck before he drove us to the house, holding my hand the entire short distance. When he stopped and killed the engine, the nerves were back. Anticipation for all that the future held. And as I let Marcel guide me, I knew that with him by my side, no matter the ups or downs, everything would be alright.

"Ready?" he whispered in my ear.

I nodded, and he slowly removed the blindfold. After blinking a few times to adjust to the brightness again, I took in the large, welcoming structure. I'd already seen the base paint job, but it dawned on me that the lettering on the sign matched the blue trim on the house. In addition, the steps leading up to the porch were each painted in a different shade of blue. Color was known to be a Victorian standard and while not over the top, I loved the pops he'd provided.

For months, he and his crew diligently worked to bring my dream alive. To bring back the house that meant so much to me. He'd even put up hanging plants like the ones my aunt used to have. I drew in a shuddered breath. "Marcel..." His name tumbled from my lips in a breathy sigh.

He wrapped his arms around my waist and rested his chin on my head. "You like it?"

"Like? Are you crazy? This is... You brought it back. She'd have loved it. *I* love it."

He trailed his fingers down my arm until he intertwined them with mine. "We have more to see. Remember that chair?" He pointed to the pair of light oak rocking chairs at the far end of the porch.

I remembered seeing something similar the day I'd gone to his workshop. The recognition must have shown on my face.

"Yes. The very same one," he confirmed. "They and the swing were made with the scraps we took out of the house during demo." Ever so softly, he circled his thumb around the palm of my hand. "Something once old, made new again, and will stand the test of time."

I leaned into him at the sentiment. It was more than the chairs, or even the house. We'd gone our separate ways, lived our separate lives, but underneath it all, our love for each other had stood the test.

I pressed a kiss to his shoulder. "Let's see the rest."

Inside, the cool AC was a welcomed relief. Not much had changed in the entry. The staircase remained the focal point. It'd been cleaned up and refinished to its former glory. Same with the trim around the wide doorways. The hardwood floors had been sanded and stained a rich, dark brown. Some people would have found all the dark wood oppressive, but I loved it. This was what it should have been, and the light cream paint on the walls complemented it perfectly.

I wandered to the right into the front parlor. The Queen Anne furniture Auntie had in the space prior had all been reupholstered, and the wood gleamed new. They'd even managed to bring the sorely neglected fireplace back to life.

The room across the foyer had my heart racing. So much time was spent in the kitchen and dining room. Auntie held council at the large farmhouse kitchen table plenty of times. I had no doubt Marcel and his team had done an amazing job, but my feet wouldn't move at the fear of how much might be different.

From where I stood, I could already see the larger cherry-wood dining table where many a holiday meal had been hosted had been replaced with smaller round ones which would allow my eventual guests more independent seating options.

Marcel rubbed small circles along my lower back, and I smiled up at him. It was going to be amazing.

Our footsteps echoed in the empty house as we made our way to the next room. The formal dining room had shrunken in size, not by a lot, but since space needed to be taken from somewhere to enlarge the kitchen, that was the room I'd sacrificed. Still, it was a comfortable location, three round tables with two chairs each and my aunt's buffet sat along the back wall. It was sparsely furnished, but I knew I had plenty to fill it with between what had been left in the house and the things I'd brought from Portland.

"Did you make all of this, too?"

He chuckled and shook his head. "No, but I did get a good deal on it from Smitty's Furniture."

"You buying stuff was not part of the plan."

He wrapped his arms around my waist and leaned in for a quick kiss. "Plans change."

"That they do."

Gripping his hand, I headed into the new kitchen. My breath hitched and my mouth went dry. It looked exactly the same for the most part, with only some minor updates. He'd somehow managed to keep the cabinets. The old butcher block counter-tops had been replaced with marble. I was in love with the new retro appliances, the forty-eight-inch stove being my favorite piece.

Out of the corner of my eye I saw my aunt's table. I walked over, ran my hand across it, and closed my fingers around my necklace.

"All I did was add a new layer of polyurethane to seal it, but no sanding or restaining. Kept it as is."

"How do you always know exactly what I need?"

Once again, I found myself cocooned in his strong arms. "I got you, baby. Will always know what you need when you need it." His confident response was completed with a sexy smile which warranted another quick kiss.

"Am I going to cry when I go upstairs?"

"If I did my job right, yes, yes you will."

He slipped his hand under my shirt. The feel of his fingers scratching against my skin helped to wipe away the impending nerves.

"I know seeing your aunt's room will be hard, but hopefully you'll love it."

I placed my hand over his heart and smiled up at him. "I have no doubt about that."

Marcel wrapped his fingers around my wrist and brought my palm to his mouth. "Let's go see the transformation."

He held my hand as we climbed the stairs. All the bedroom

doors were closed, and each had a different bird attached to carry on the bird theme. I wasn't surprised to see that Auntie's room was the Blue Jay. Marcel opened the door, and I closed my eyes for a moment to steady myself before taking it all in. The fact that her furniture was gone knocked the breath out of my lungs. I'd know it wouldn't be there. I'd not wanted people using it, but still to see it replaced jarred me momentarily.

Marcel squeezed my hand. His reassurance reminded me this was a good thing. Reminding me she'd have loved what it had become. Silent tears rolled down my cheeks. An exciting new path in my life with an amazing man beside me for each step.

Emotion thickened my throat when I entered the bathroom. The light blue tiles I'd picked out were beautiful, but the decorative tile blue jay in the niche...that was another one of those surprises where he'd gone above and beyond. Adding personal touches that had so much meaning and for no other reason than because he loved me.

35

MARCEL

Cynthia wiped the tears from her cheeks. This reveal meant more to me than any other client ever had or would. Each sigh, smile, gasp, and even the tears pulled at my heart. I moved up behind her, resting my hands on her shoulders while absent-mindedly providing her with a soft massage.

"I take it you like the tile work?"

"It's beautiful," she whispered.

Pride and joy swelled at her words. I'd wanted this to be special for her. To honor her aunt's memory. To make sure the house, and more importantly this room, were something that made her happy. I'd known she'd get emotional as we toured the house, and I'd given the crew the day off even though we still had some minor things to finish up.

Cynthia's first walk-through needed to be a private event, and part of me was being a little selfish. I didn't want to share these intimate moments with additional prying eyes or ears.

"I guarantee this will be the most sought out room once you open. Not saying the other two aren't nice, but this room...it's special, and your guests will feel that."

She reached back and covered my hand with her own. "Are

you saying that because you did all the work in here?" The humor in her voice brought a grin to my face.

"What can I say, baby, I'm damn good at what I do."

She turned and slipped her arms around my neck, and I rested mine on her waist while letting my hands hold onto her ass. Her eyes were red, and her lashes were wet, but happiness radiated through her entire being. Knowing I had a part in that warmed my soul and made me want to spend my every waking moment trying to recreate that feeling in her.

Cynthia stretched up, and I met her for the kiss. Her soft lips were salty from the tears. Before I could get too lost in her, she pulled back.

"You are very good at what you do."

The coy smile and playful wink drew a groan from the back of my throat. Another quick squeeze of her ass then I stepped away to put some space between us.

"We have two more rooms, plus your owner's suite. Stop trying to distract me."

She tilted her head and dropped her gaze to my crotch for a moment. "I'm sure there are plenty of sturdy surfaces up there."

I could only shake my head. We'd spent nearly every night together, and I loved it. I didn't even mind that she stole the covers and took up seventy-five percent of my California king because she liked having her side plus the middle of the bed. Waking up with her every morning was worth the sacrifice. And as a bonus, we'd tested the sturdiness of my bed, couch, and kitchen table and chairs so far.

The Cardinal and Hummingbird rooms also now boasted their own bathrooms, though smaller than the Blue Jay suite, but large enough the guests would still be comfortable. Considering we took the house from a three-bedroom, one bathroom to a three-bedroom, three bathroom—not including the owner's suite—and we managed to keep all the charm and make the new additions look as if they'd always been part of the home was an accomplishment I was proud of.

We headed to the end of the hall to the back staircase, now enclosed with drywall and sealed off with a new, old door. The entry to her space. I wouldn't let myself get too disappointed over the fact that she'd no longer be splitting her time between my house and Regina's now that we'd finished. Wanting to sleep under her own roof was more than understandable, and if she'd have me, I'd lay my head wherever hers was.

I turned the glass handle and opened the door. "Ladies first."

My heart rate sped up as I climbed the stairs behind her. This was the final piece. The last thing to make her dream a reality. At the top of the landing, Cynthia gasped and covered her mouth with her hands. The usable attic space was only about seven hundred square feet, but it had soaring ceilings, which added to the airiness.

"Oh, Marcel..." The whispered astonishment in her voice was all the affirmation I needed.

The open area that was to be her living room remained unfurnished because she had her items from Portland she wanted to use. To the left was the small but well-appointed galley style kitchen. Cynthia glided over to the island and released a low sigh as she ran her fingers over the polished and sealed live-edge countertop.

"I can't believe...how...this is more than I ever expected. And the turret. You made me a breakfast nook in the turret."

From the outside of the house, the window had merely been decorative, but once we started construction up here and determined the layout, I knew it would be the perfect spot for a small table and built-in bench.

Cynthia curled up on the light blue cushion and rested her head against the glass. Her shoulders relaxed and she closed her eyes while stroking her aunt's necklace. I strolled over to join her, leaning against the wall. The view was beautiful with the trees and expansive yard. There was no way in hell this place—Cynthia—wouldn't be a success.

She unfolded herself and eased into my arms. "This is all so beautiful. Thank you."

"No thanks needed, baby. This project was all from the heart."

She pressed her lips to my neck. "That just means more thanks is needed."

I squeezed her ass. "Hmm, whatcha got in mind?"

She grabbed mine in return. "Depends on if you made my shower as nice as yours."

"Ha. Not a chance. Told you I needed some reason to get you back to my place from time to time."

"Fine," she said in a dramatic sigh. "But it better be close."

I took her hand and headed back to the living area to the walled off rooms. "And behind door number two..."

She stepped inside and did a little dance at the sight of her bathroom. Off-white arabesque tiles ran up the entire tub and shower area. There wasn't enough room for a separate soaker tub like at my house, but I made sure to get her a nice deep one that would fit. The half-glass partition kept the space from feeling closed in. And while she didn't have as many body jets, I'd managed to work in three.

"Is that the linen closet?" She pointed to the pocket door at the end of the tub.

My heart rate spiked again, and I rubbed the back of my neck. On the other side would be the final piece to hopefully make everything complete.

"No, that would be door number one that we passed. It leads into your bedroom. I wanted you to have an en suite, but also if you did have people up here, you wouldn't want them walking through your room to get to the bathroom."

"You are more than just a pretty face."

I held my breath when she opened it.

Floral arrangements of daisies and roses sat on the dresser and nightstands that had been downstairs. And in the middle of the room, her aunt's four-poster bed to complete the set.

"I knew you wouldn't want to give it away. And since you love mine so much, I got you the same type of mattress."

She didn't acknowledge my words. Her attention seemed to be focused on the silver tray in the middle of the unmade bed. Atop it was a tiny treasure chest box.

"What's all this?" Wonder and bewilderment colored her tone as she slowly moved forward.

"My way of saying welcome home."

I moved past her and retrieved the container. All the words I'd rehearsed seemed to be stuck in my throat. All the dreams I'd had when we were eighteen were contained in the light object in my hands.

"What is that? My keys?"

I shook my head. "Not quite." I took a breath. "Cynthia Marshall, I love you..."

"Yes."

I startled then laughed. "Can't let me get the question out?"

She shook her head. "No. We've lived our lives separately and now I'm ready to live one jointly."

"Woman, you are stealing my thunder."

I opened the lid and showed her the ring.

"Oh my..."

My hands shook as I freed the small brown circle and placed it on her finger. "It's made from oak and the wildflowers that are epoxied in are from the yard. It's durable and should stand the test of time. Like us."

"You made it?"

"Yes. But I know diamonds are a girl's best friend so we can go shopping and you can pick out something you will love."

She looked at the ring on her finger then circled her arms around my neck. "I already have."

Thank you for purchasing and reading! I hope you enjoyed Renovation of Love. If you can spare a few more moments of your time, I'd greatly appreciate if you'd leave a review.

If you'd like to get an extra HEA scene with Cynthia and Marcel you can sign up and get the bonus here: https://BookHip.com/KFQZNWD

Regina's story, Heat of Love will be out in June. Please enjoy this sneak peek.

HEAT OF LOVE

IT WAS SURREAL TO WATCH EVERYTHING YOU'D WORKED FOR, everything your family had built and dedicated their lives to for over four generations, be taken from you. Even from across the street, the heat from the flames warmed my skin. I'd never understood what people meant when they'd say they had an out of body experience, but that had to be what I was having. But none of it seemed real. It couldn't be real.

People were shouting. Sirens blared. A crackle and hiss as more flames sparked and lit up the night sky like a cruel firework display. Somewhere that sounded both far off and extremely close a person screamed and cried out in disbelief.

This wasn't happening.

This *wasn't* happening.

There was pressure on my hand. Other voices were trying to cut through the cries.

"Regina!"

"Regina!"

My name, someone was calling my name. I turned to the left and saw Cynthia running toward me. More pressure on my hand. It was momma. She was crying into daddy's shoulder while holding tight to me.

Cynthia threw her arms around my shoulders. "Oh god, Regina. What happened?"

She put her palms on my cheeks. They were cold. So cold in comparison to how hot it was. Shouting. So much shouting and questions—too many questions. I opened my mouth to speak, to answer the unanswerable, but no words came. A long soul shattering scream ripped from my throat as reality sank in.

It was gone.

I OPENED my eyes and quickly closed them again against the bright sunlight. I was home, in my bed. *How did I get home?* There was movement beside me and I looked over to find Cynthia curled up and sleeping peacefully. Last time I'd woken to find her sleeping beside me had been after the accident.

Once again, my lids fluttered shut as last night's events replayed in my head. I tried to take in a breath, but couldn't fully inflate my lungs.

It was gone.

Emptiness spread through me as the thought squeezed my heart. I swung my legs over the side of the bed and pushed into a sitting position. Cynthia startled at the movement.

"Hey. You okay? You need something?" Her voice was groggy with sleep, but she was up and beside me rubbing her eyes.

I could only shake my head and will the tears burning the back of my eyes to stay put. They didn't listen.

She wrapped her arms around my shoulders and held me tight, rocking us gently. "It's going to be okay. It will all be okay."

"How did this happen?"

"I don't know, but we'll figure it out and then we'll rebuild."

I sat up and wiped the tears from my cheeks. "Thanks for being here."

"Not a single thanks needed. You go shower and I'll get breakfast started if Marcel hasn't."

I frowned. "Marcel?"

"Yeah, he slept in Darnell's room, and your parents are in the guest room."

I massaged my temples hoping to stave off the quickly building headache. More flashes from last night of momma crying with daddy trying to console her. How did this happen on my watch? I was sure Big Momma and Nana were rolling over in their graves knowing what I let happen to their pride and joy.

"How is Momma? The stress is not good for either of them."

Cynthia nodded. "She was concerned about you. We all were."

I let out a heavy sigh. "It doesn't seem real, you know?"

"I know. I texted Irene. She'll probably call later today. She was going to see if she could rearrange her patients, but if not, she'll be here Saturday. And your daddy got in touch with Darnell who was ready to drive home last night. So, expect to see him soon."

Mention of my baby boy—who was now more a man—brought a smile to my face. Though I'd mostly adjusted to being an empty-nester, I still looked forward to his visits. However, our family business being in ruins was not a reason I'd want him coming to see me.

I rolled my shoulders in a failed attempt to release some tension and glanced at the clock. Unease made my stomach ache. I should have been heading to the bakery, preparing for the day, instead I sat with my friend who rubbed small circles on my back and an absolute loss of purpose covering me like a wet blanket.

"I'm going to shower then I need to go...I need to see."

"Okay. We'll go with you."

I squeezed her hand as emotion clogged my throat. There was zero use in arguing with her over her need to not babysit me. My friend had already seen me at my worst sixteen years ago. With her and Irene I didn't have to worry about being strong and pulled together all the time. I pushed off the bed and padded over to my bathroom.

As the water heated up, I rested my palms on the granite countertop and stared at my reflection. The bags under my bloodshot eyes seemed to be packed for a month-long trip. I'd survived the loss of my husband and the near loss of my son.

"This will not beat me," I hissed to my reflection.

And it would not. My heart ached and my soul was crushed, but this would not beat me. I'd always handled my business. This would not beat me.

After my shower I went through my normal routine including my makeup. I may have had nowhere to go, but I needed some normalcy. Something to help remind myself of my new mantra: this would not beat me.

Voices carried down the hall, reminding me I wouldn't have to deal with things alone. The scent of coffee and sausage made my stomach growl.

Dad spotted me first. "Morning, sweetheart." He walked over and gave me a hug and kissed my cheek.

He ushered me to the table where Cynthia and Marcel sat. Momma put a plate in front of me and patted my arm before she gathered the empty dishes.

"Has anyone seen my phone?" I asked, after taking a bite of eggs

There were calls to make and I needed to talk to the insurance company. Rebuilding couldn't get underway until they paid out and I knew the red tape would be a bitch.

"It might still be in the car," Marcel answered. He pushed back from the table, kissed my friend on the top of her head and then went outside.

I grinned at her. "Have I told you lately how glad I am you came to your senses?"

She rolled her eyes. "Really. This is what you want to bring up?"

I shrugged. "Momma agrees with me."

On cue mom chimed in. "Yes you snatched Madison's most eligible bachelor."

Dad turned in his chair, his thick eyebrows pulled in a deep V. "What am I chopped liver?"

"Man please. You ain't been a bachelor since the Stone Age." She walked up behind him and wrapped her arms around his neck. "Just the way I like it."

He turned and gave her a quick kiss. "Damn right."

This was perfect. A tiny bubble of normal that could almost make me forget. Almost.

Marcel returned, with his son in tow, and set my dead cell-phone next to my plate. MJ greeted us and offered his sympathies and assurances they'd get the place up and running when the time came, before he left with his father.

After Cynthia excused herself to go get ready, Momma sat beside me and wrapped her arms around my shoulders. "I can tell you're blamin' yourself."

My stomach churned and the throbbing in my head increased. "How can I not? First all that crap with Trent and now this." Just speaking that man's name made my blood pressure spike.

I was still having a hard time wrapping my head around the fact a man we'd trusted, that *I'd* trusted, had stolen from me. I'd considered him more than an employee; he was a friend. I'd listened to the family, caved on not doing it all on my own. Given him more responsibility and he'd returned that kindness by forging orders and skimming off the top. Right under my nose. I couldn't help but to feel like an inept idiot for not only failing to catch it sooner, but for not even suspecting it was happening in the first place. Things were just starting to settle from that after the arrest and now my bakery had caught fire.

"Don't let that thievin', lyin' bastard take up your energy," Dad spat.

He was mostly removed from the business other than to offer support and encouragement. And be first in line as a taste tester for new recipes. But that didn't mean he stayed out of the loop. He may have been a retired postal worker, but the bakery was a family business.

"Exactly what your father said. And as for the fire, we can't predict these things. It might have been some faulty gas line, or dry lightning. We just can't say. Either way it's out of your control."

I knew they were right, but that didn't stop the self-deprecating thoughts. I was at the helm and needed to protect it until my niece Trisha was ready to take over. We would rebuild, and the legacy would continue. I didn't care what it took.

"Cynthia is going to go with me to the bakery, then we'll pop over to the fire station to see if Chief Morris can give me some info. I'm gonna need it for the insurance I'm guessin'. And the sooner we know the sooner we can file our claim and get back at it."

"Do you want us to come?" Dad asked. "You know Pat and I are fishing buddies."

"I know, Daddy. But I'm a big girl and I can handle it."

"You sure? Not that I don't think he'd be straight with you, but you know how men are," Momma said.

"I feel like I should take some offense here," he grumbled, shifting back and forth in his seat.

"Oh please." She waved him off.

"Ready when you are," Cynthia announced on her return.

"I got it. But if I think he's giving me the run around, I'll let you ride in and save me." I hugged him tight and took momentary solace in his embrace. "Lock up when you leave." I kissed momma on the cheek then headed out to survey the damage.

Pre-order available. Coming June 21, 2021

ABOUT THE AUTHOR

Meka James is a writer of adult contemporary and erotic romance. A born and raised Georgia Peach, she still resides in the southern state with her hubby of 16 years and counting. Mom to four kids of the two legged variety, she also has four fur-babies of the canine variety. Leo the turtle and Spade the snake rounds out her wacky household. When not writing or reading, Meka can be found playing The Sims 3, sometimes Sims 4, and making up fun stories to go with the pixelated people whose world she controls.

https://www.authormekajames.com/

OTHER BOOKS BY MEKA

Fiendish: A Twisted Fairytale

please note this book tackles dark themes that may be upsetting to readers. You don't have to read Fiendish to read and enjoy Not Broken

Not Broken: The Happily Ever After

*Continuation of Calida's story from Fiendish

The Lists

*Extended HEA for Calida and Malcolm from Not Broken

Anything Once

*Erotic romance featuring Ian and Quinn Faraday who are on a journey to spice up their sex lives

Desert Rose Hook-ups series

Being Neighborly

Being Hospitable

Being Cordial

www.ingramcontent.com/pod-product-compliance
Lightning Source LLC
Chambersburg PA
CBHW032024120726
47898CB00002BB/656